I was so confused. Evan made me happy—right? But I couldn't just let Cody disappear from my life. Why couldn't I decide?

"Cody?" I said when I couldn't stand the silence any longer. "Are you mad?"

He glanced at me, his eyes flashing. "Why would I be mad?" he growled.

"He just kind of showed up last night," I said.

"Don't," he said. "I don't want to know."

"I just want to tell you that I've been thinking about you, us—"

"And he just showed up and spent the night last night. I hear you." Cody swung around a corner so forcefully that I gathered the cria more tightly into my arms to keep it from sliding.

"Please, give me another chance," I said. "I'm not ready to let you go."

"But you're not ready to let him go, either," Cody said. Pain was sharp in his voice.

"Please," I said. "Give me whatever time limit you want. I'll follow it. But let me figure this out in my own way until then." I was afraid to touch him, so I clutched the baby animal to my chest and hoped.

He looked at me hard again, but his eyes softened before he looked back at the road. He made a turn into a parking lot and switched off the key. He turned to me and looked into my eyes. "A week," he said. "One torturous week, and I'm done."

She thinks moving to a ranch will lead to the simple life she craves, but the countryside has other ideas...

After divorcing her unfaithful husband, Meg Taylor buys an alpaca ranch to finally do something on her own. Almost as soon as she arrives, she meets not one, but two, handsome—and baffling—men. She thinks choosing between the shy veterinarian and her charming securities co-worker is her biggest problem, until life and death on the ranch make her re-evaluate more than her love life. At least her new life is nothing like her old one.

KUDOS for *Fuzzy Logic*

In *Fuzzy Logic* by Maren Anderson, Megan Taylor is recently divorced from her cheating scum of a husband. She finds her life and home in California too painful, after finding her husband in the shower with the housekeeper, and moves to an alpaca ranch in Oregon. No sooner does she arrive than she has not one but two gorgeous men fighting over her. My kind of love triangle. Meg knows that she can only have one, as she doesn't want to hurt anyone as she has been hurt, but which one to choose? She's afraid to commit to either, in case she picks the wrong one. The story has a strong plot, with several subplots and a spicy romance, that heats up the pages. It also has some spine-tingling tension that has nothing to do with sex. ~ *Taylor Jones, Reviewer*

Fuzzy Logic by Maren Anderson is a cute clever romantic suspense. Our heroine, Megan Taylor, longs for the simple quiet life after her divorce from her husband, who she found taking a shower with their college-age housekeeper. And he wasn't helping her clean the walls, either. So Megan quits her job as a securities advisor in the Bay Area in California and buys an alpaca ranch in Oregon. Now I've never seen an alpaca, but Anderson makes them sound adorable. The two men who vie for Megan's attention are also adorable—if you can call hunks adorable. Evan is Megan's co-worker at her new securities job. He's charming, handsome, confident, and pursues Megan aggressively. Cody, on the hand, is a shy veterinarian, also a hunk, but backs away when he thinks she wants Evan. But Megan doesn't know what she wants and she's running out of time to find out. Anderson has crafted an exciting and heartwarming tale that immerses one in the quiet country life of rural Oregon, which turns out not to be so quiet after all. A great read. ~ *Regan Murphy, Reviewer*

ACKNOWLEDGEMENTS

Thank you to the team at Black Opal Books and to Kate Ristau, a writer and friend who blazes the trail.

Fuzzy Logic

Maren Anderson

A Black Opal Books Publication

GENRE: ROMANTIC SUSPENSE/WESTERN ROMANCE

FUZZY LOGIC
Copyright © 2015 by Maren Anderson
Cover Design by Maren Anderson
All cover art copyright © 2015
All Rights Reserved
Print ISBN: 978-1-626943-73-5

First Publication: DECEMBER 2015

Published by Black Opal Books **http://www.blackopalbooks.com**

DEDICATION

For my family, especially my husband,
who is nearly as crazy about animals as I am.

Prologue

June, two years ago:

The rain rattled the tin porch roof at Nana's farm as I stood and waited for her to open the door. I was clammy from wrestling my bag out of the trunk in the downpour and bone tired from everything else. Nana didn't say anything when she saw me, just opened the screen door wider and stepped aside so I could drag in my suitcase.

Nana was just as good at *not* talking as she was at talking. She didn't ask me a single question until I was dry and warmed up in her kitchen, breathing in the aroma of her coffee and the smell of her biscuits. Biting into one—warm and soft as love smeared with jam—instantly reminded me why I'd driven all this way to be with her.

"Boysenberry?" I asked, holding up the biscuit.

"Mixed with blackberry," Nana said. "Won a blue at the fair last summer."

We smiled at each other.

"Is everything okay?" she asked, knowing, of course, that I wouldn't arrive unannounced if things were okay.

"I found Martin in the shower with the girl who cleans the house."

"I see," she said. "I take it he wasn't helping her scrub."

I laughed and cried at the same time. I felt Nana wrap me up in her arms and knead my knotted shoulders like bread. She kissed my head as if I were five.

Chapter 1

April, this year:

I sat at a crossroads with my blinker on while I poked at the GPS on my dashboard. The dulcet-toned voice murmured again, "Turn left onto Smith Road."

Turn left? Left of me was a gravel road that disappeared under a canopy of fir trees. It did not look familiar at all.

The pickup behind me beeped politely, so I took a deep breath and turned down the road toward my new home.

"How could I have forgotten the way in a month?" I asked the GPS.

The pristine tires of my new SUV crunched on the unfamiliar surface. I crept along the road because someone once told me that driving on gravel was like driving on ice: your brakes were basically useless. Every time I turned the wheel, I imagined myself careening into a ditch or taking out someone's mailbox.

"Proceed for one-point-four miles," the lady on my dash purred.

One-point-four *miles*? This was going to take forever. I drummed my thumbs on the steering wheel, but I didn't dare go any faster.

After what must have been many more than 1.4 miles, the GPS binged. "You have arrived at your destination."

I took my foot off the gas and coasted to a stop. There was nothing in front of me but a long, blank gravel road. I stabbed the screen with my finger, succeeding not in making her explain herself, but only in knocking the device off of the dash and into the foot well. "You have arrived!" she called from the floor.

I eased the car forward another fifty feet, and I finally recognized the tiny sign hanging from a tree branch: *Alpine Alpacas*. I turned up the drive, giggling to myself.

At first, spindly fir trees flanked the driveway and blocked the view, but soon they thinned out, and the single-lane driveway straightened. I slammed on the brakes when I saw the house.

The picture I'd seen of the on the realty website must have been taken from that very spot. Before me spread ten acres of pasture, peppered with brown, black and white dots—my alpacas. Atop a little hill overlooking the grass was my house, white with green shutters and a long porch. Next to it sat a red barn.

I started my SUV—which the salesman had assured me would tackle any terrain I was likely to encounter—up the steepest part of the gravel drive and wondered exactly what terrain he had been thinking of. The car certainly had second thoughts about the gravel.

I parked on the concrete driveway pad next to the house and tried to calm the SUV's nerves by stroking the dashboard and cooing, "It's okay. I'm sure the road won't be as steep or gravelly next time." When I looked up, I caught a white-haired man grinning at me from outside my window. I'd only talked to Lew briefly when I visited the ranch, but I recognized his smile instantly. He was tall and wiry, barely filling out his overalls. A dirty ball cap sat far back on his head, and he was chewing on the end of a pipe. I don't think anyone could look more country than Lew.

I opened my door and stuck out my hand. "Lew!"

"Glad you found the place on your own." He shook my hand and then winked. "Your car okay?"

I waved indifferently at the car. "He'll be fine, big baby." I smacked the fender as if it were a lovable dumb animal.

Lew nodded. "This is Molly."

She had been examining the new tires and unscathed paint of the SUV. I stuck out my hand and was rewarded with a shake as crushing as any man's.

"Hi!" I squeaked in pain.

"Hello," Molly said and pumped my hand exactly once.

Her ball cap was just as dirty as Lew's and, though

she was at least a decade younger and probably out-weighed him by thirty pounds, they were obviously a team. She was as much a part of the ranch as he was. She wore her dirty-blonde hair in a long braid down her back, and she hated me.

She squinted into the distance over my shoulder and said, "Excuse me." Then she stalked off to the barn.

I blinked after her. "Is she mad at me?"

Lew pushed his ball cap to the back of his head. He took so long to answer that I had time to notice his hat had a tractor on the front. "No," he said finally. "She and the guy who owned this place were friends. The way his divorce played out really upset Molly. It's not you."

"Oh." We watched Molly disappear into the barn. "I'm glad I don't have to win you over," I said.

"Well, we'll have to see about that, won't we?" Then he slapped me on the back. "Let me help you with your bags."

The inside of the house was just as charming as I re-membered, though now it was empty. We walked through the tiled mudroom where Lew kicked off his work boots.

"You don't have to do that," I said.

He chuckled. "Yes, I do. They don't call these 'shit kickers' for nothing."

The house echoed like a cavern. None of my furni-ture had arrived, and we walked through the living room with its stark hardwood, the kitchen with its cold granite, and the dining room with its bead-board wainscoting. The place seemed too big and too small all at once, without my stuff, or any stuff, in it. I peeked into the spare bedrooms, and they were chilly cubes of nothing. I realized I was chewing my thumbnail, so I shoved my hands in my pocket.

I opened the door to the master bedroom and sighed in relief. The new bed I had ordered had been delivered. I figured I deserved a new bed after everything, and I had picked the softest, most opulent mattress I could find. I had been fantasizing about sleeping, luxuriating, in my new bed in my new house in my new life ever since I signed the offer on the ranch. Now, Lew set my bags down in the bedroom next to the bed, which stood alone in the middle of the room, all set up with its sleigh-bed head and footboards, minus any sheets or pillows.

"Shit," I said.

"What?"

"I kind of forgot that when you buy a bed, it doesn't come all made up."

Lew looked like he was going to pop with mirth. "Funny thing."

"Guess I'll go shopping tonight."

"I could lend you a sleeping bag, Miss."

"Call me Meg." I shook my head. "Thanks anyway. I've been on the road all day, and I really want to sleep in my new bed on some new sheets. After we look around outside, I'll just hop in the car and go someplace nearby."

"Okay." There was his lopsided smile again. "Meg."

We walked to the living room and stepped out through the sliding glass door onto the porch. I took a deep breath of springtime air.

The porch had a roof like Nana's, and I wondered if it made the same sound in the rain.

"So, you like the house?" Lew asked.

"Oh, yes. In Berkeley, we were all piled on top of each other. Even though we had our own house, we couldn't get away from the neighbors."

"We?"

"We—my ex-husband and me," I said. "There is no 'we' anymore. It's just a habit."

"Ah." Lew looked out over the fields. "Do you want to meet the critters now?"

I smiled. "Yes. Yes, I do."

Lew led the way across the lawn to the fence, which was made of seven plain wires running along posts. He pointed to the top and the bottom two wires. "Those are hot," he said. "Electrified. Just to keep the other critters out. Still, don't touch them." With that, he parted two of the middle wires and ducked his head under, swinging first one leg and then the other through.

I just stood there.

"You want me to climb through an electric fence?" I looked down at my Berkeley sweatshirt, crisp new jeans, and blue Vans sneakers. I remembered that I had considered wearing pumps today.

Lew's face looked like it might split from grinning, but he held the wires apart for me. "Just put one leg through, then your head, then the other leg. You won't get zapped. I promise."

I followed his directions, hoping my clumsy gene didn't make an appearance. Mercifully, I stood up to find myself in a verdant pasture with twenty pairs of eyes watching me. I followed Lew down the hill until we were a few feet from them.

Then he held up his hand. "Sit down."

I looked down at the damp grass. "What?"

"On the ground, Miss—Meg," he said. "They'll get real curious if you sit down."

To prove his point, Lew plonked down in the pasture. Instantly, three alpacas broke from the staring herd and walked up to him for a good sniff.

"Oh, right."

I sat, after making sure I wasn't putting my bottom on anything worse than wet grass. As soon as my ass started feeling damp, a little pod of alpacas—a brown, a white, and a black—broke from the herd and walked up the hill toward me, long necks low and stretched out, velvet noses twitching, little spear-ears pointed up and out of their fuzzy topknots. One of them hummed at me inquisitively. They stopped at arms' length and regarded me. I stretched out a hand. They spun and ran three steps away. These creatures weren't nearly as friendly as my pair of alpacas, which lived at Nana's farm. For the first time since I saw the ranch online, a wave of doubt made me shudder. I looked at Lew.

"Just sit still now," he said. "They're not dogs or cats even. Eventually, they'll trust you, but you've got to earn it."

As if to mock me a little, one of the alpacas that had greeted Lew flopped down next to him on its belly and chewed cud as he rubbed its back.

I looked back at my welcoming committee, which had begun to creep back toward me while I wasn't paying attention. I put my hands under my wet butt and smiled at them.

A black stepped forward and stretched its neck long and low. "Hmm?" it said.

Then it stepped closer, within reach, but I kept my hands where they were. Finally, a little black nose touched mine and blew gently. I blew back. The alpaca sneezed and threw up its head, but then it came back for another round.

"You've been granted an alpaca kiss!" cried Lew. "Congratulations! You're now officially hooked."

"I sure am," I said quietly as the other two alpacas came up for their kisses, too.

The first pasture turned out to be the maternity ward.

"We like to keep the pregnant girls and babies close to the house," Lew said.

"Makes sense."

"Let's go see the other critters."

We climbed through more fences, meeting the open girls—"open" means unbred, I learned—and the young males who were wrestling in their pasture.

"Shriek like banshees when they fight," Lew said. "And in the middle of the night. Don't let it scare you."

"Really?" I watched the boys rear up and shove each other around with their chests. Apart from a little grunting, I didn't hear any noise. "I'll take your word for it."

The boys that weren't fighting saw Lew and ran to him. They shoved their noses in his pockets, so he pulled out baby carrots and managed to give each animal only one.

"Spoiled, aren't they?" he said. He rumpled the top-knot on one white animal, and it butted him.

"Come on," Lew said. "Let's go see his majesty."

The stud barn sat in a far pasture, trim and dainty compared to the larger barn by the house. A number of alpacas grazed in the pasture, five or six brown and gray and white animals. As soon as we stepped through the fence, a huge black shadow shot from the barn and bounded toward us.

"Hey, Basso!" Lew called as the alpaca slowed to a stop in front of him and started looking for carrots. "Mr. Ambassador must have his treats."

"He's huge!"

Mr. Ambassador could look me in the eye. While I'm not tall, the other alpacas I'd met only made it to my chin.

"Feel his fleece," Lew said. He wrapped an arm around the beast's neck and fed him a carrot.

I plunged my hands into six inches of the softest, silkiest fleece I'd ever felt. I pulled the fleece open like a book and saw little ladders of wave marching down to his skin.

"Gorgeous crimp, huh?" Lew said.

"I can't believe the color!"

Mr. Ambassador was inky, light-swallowing black all the way down to his skin. I thought of how awesome it would feel to knit it into a luscious scarf or sweater.

"Yeah. He's a special guy," Lew said. "I call him

'Basso.' Seems to fit him. He was born here, you know."

"Was he shown?"

"He won everything there was to win," Lew said. He pointed to the other alpacas in the field. "These are all his dates—the girls who are here waiting to be bred to him."

"Oh. I can see why." I slid my hand down his back in the dense fleece and let my fingers trail off his tail. That's when he kicked me in the shin so hard I fell.

"Meg!" Lew was at my side and Basso was running back to his harem.

"Just a bruise," I said. "I'm okay."

He pulled me to my feet. "Damn. I forgot to warn you about his tail. I'm sorry."

"It's okay." I stood and pressed the heel of my hand into my tender shin. "He kicks high."

"Alpacas are like cows. They can kick in any direction," he said. "I've been kicked by cows, horses, sheep, all sorts of hard-footed critters. I'll take the soft feet of an alpaca any day."

"Yeah, you're right," I said. "I was kicked by a horse when I was seventeen. Missed my prom because I was in traction."

"Ow." Lew looked at Basso and shook his head. "That one is just all hormones and no brains." He squinted at the barn. "You okay?" he asked. "I think I see a gate open."

"I'm fine."

When he was out of earshot, I sat down and took some deep breaths. I couldn't hold it together anymore.

The horse that broke my leg had been trying to kill

me. No one had told me that the newly rescued horse had been beaten with a rake by his abusive owner. When I stepped into his stall to clean it as I had done hundreds of times before with other horses, he kicked me so hard I was flung against the wall and knocked unconscious. My friends were able to get me out of there, but they thought I was dead. I woke up in the hospital.

Basso had kicked me in the same leg, and it ached to the bone. *What the hell are you doing here?* I asked myself. *What made you think you could do this alone?*

I choked down my doubt and smiled when Lew came back.

"How're you doing?" he asked, helping me up again.

"I'm fine," I said. "Like you said, Basso isn't a horse."

"Then let's go see the girls."

Lew took me up to the "ladies' barn," where the dams were housed. It was a huge building by Berkeley standards, but compared to even Nana and Poppy's barn, it was petite. It was only one story for starters, and it could be configured for eight stalls, but it was only set up to divide the girls into their four pastures. It smelled exactly the way a barn should: hay, manure, animals. The scents triggered memories—the way that smells do—of sitting in Nana and Poppy's barn, enjoying the cool shade and watching Poppy fiddle with some piece of antiquated equipment.

It was his purpose in life to resurrect broken machines of all kinds, and seeing him coax life back into a radio or combine harvester while I chewed on a sun-hot apple or piece of hay was as calming as a day at the spa. I know. I've tried both.

This barn also had storage across the aisle from the stalls, and that was where we found Molly attaching a wagon to the tractor.

"Molly's going out to scoop poop," Lew said. "The alpacas all use communal dung piles, and we just go clean up after them a couple times a week."

"Communal dung piles?"

"They all poop in the same spot," Molly said, slamming a pin into a bolt on the trailer. "Geesh. How much do you know about alpacas, anyway?"

I felt myself blush, and was instantly angry with myself for it. I didn't have to explain to this bitter woman that I had noticed my own alpacas pooping in the same spot and wondered about it. Despite being angry, I said, "I don't know as much as you, Molly, but I am here to learn."

"Oh?" Molly said, raising an eyebrow. I had always wanted to be able to cock a brow like that. "Wanna come poop scoopin'? You can ride there." She pointed to a tiny ledge behind the seat and wheels.

"I—I can't today, Molly," I stammered. "I need to buy sheets before the stores close."

"Suit yourself." Molly started the tractor. Its roaring clatter effectively ended the conversation.

Lew clenched the pipe in his teeth and put a hand on my shoulder. "Molly will come around," he said when she drove away.

"I hope so."

Then Lew smiled and turned to the door of the barn. "Here's some sunshine," he said.

"What do you mean?"

He cupped a hand to his ear. "Listen."

I did the same and frowned when I didn't hear anything. Lew shushed me before I could complain, so I listened more. Then I heard the crunch of tires on gravel.

Lew nodded. "You'll get real good at hearing tires," he said. "There's no traffic, so any car coming is coming to see us."

We stepped out of the barn to see a blue pickup racing up the driveway, kicking up a rooster tail of gravel and mud.

"Who's that?"

"That's the vet," Lew said.

"Why's he in such a hurry?"

"Hurry? That's slow for him."

The pickup slowed a bit for the turn to the barn, but I still stepped back as it skidded to a stop in front of us. Lew went up to the truck and leaned on the hood as the vet collected his things and threw the door open.

"Hi, Lew," he said. "How's things?"

The two men shook hands like old friends, but they were quite a contrast in manhood. Lew was white-haired and willowy, the vet jet-haired and broad-shouldered. They both looked like they belonged on a ranch. I felt out of place, like a new pair of shoes, fresh out of the box, that shouldn't be dirty yet. I absently put my hand on my damp bottom.

"Who's this?"

"Cody, meet Meg Taylor, new owner of Alpine Alpacas."

"Hi," I said.

"This is Dr. Cody Arden," Lew said.

"Nice to meet you," Dr. Arden said, shaking my hand.

He had a soft hand and gentle grip. Lew's hand was hard and horny with calluses. I smiled.

"I'm just here to follow up on a couple things." He smiled and his brown eyes crinkled. "Nothing to worry about."

I didn't realize I was holding the vet's hand and grinning stupidly until Lew cleared his throat and said, "Meg was saying she needed to go buy some sheets."

I snatched my hand away. "Oh, yeah. To sleep in." Then I blushed like a twelve-year-old.

Dr. Cody Arden put his hands in his pockets. "Is that so? Well, you'd better get a move on. Things close early around here. Lew and I can take care of things."

"Oh, okay," I said. "Nice meeting you." I walked off toward my car, wondering what had just happened to me. Blushing? I never blush, yet my face still felt hot.

Then it occurred to me that, as the owner of the animals the vet was here to see, I should at least inquire which ones he was going to check. Instead of walking back and asking, though, I stopped and watched Lew and Dr. Arden laugh about something. They knocked each other back and forth as they moseyed into the barn.

The hard-wired aversion to shame deep inside me said, *There's a chance they are laughing because your pants are wet. Stop gawking, get in your car, and go shopping.*

So, I did.

I grabbed my purse from the counter in the mudroom and counted to ten so I could walk to my car with some poise, despite my wet butt. No one was watching, of course, but you never knew. Maybe I impressed the squirrel with my nonchalance. When I was safely in my car, I rubbed the tired out of my eyes. Then I started the engine and chanted, "Sheets, sheets, sheets," to focus myself as I crept down the gravel road toward town.

I didn't want to admit it to Lew, but after the tour, I was already overwhelmed. Lew said there were between twenty to thirty alpacas on the ranch at any one time, depending on how many were visiting Basso. The alpacas were wonderful, and I promised myself that I would sit in the pasture with them once a day for the rest of my life.

But the number of alpacas wasn't the worrisome part. It was the business. Selling breedings and animals, advertising, buying hay, making something with the fleece—it was a full-time job running the ranch, and, I realized I'd eventually have to take it over. For now, Lew and Molly ran the place, and I was so grateful that they lived in the single-wide trailer behind the barn—it was the original dwelling on the property—and worked for their rent. Even though my new mantra was "I'll do it by myself," I wasn't insane enough to try to learn how to run a ranch completely on my own.

At least the vet was friendly.

I sighed and turned on the seat warmers, hoping they

would dry my pants. I searched my GPS for a menu labeled "shopping," but it listed nothing when I tapped it. I tried it again. And again. Finally, I took it out of its holder and shook it, hollering, "I just want to go to Nordstrom and buy sheets!"

I hurled it into the passenger seat and headed back toward the last town I'd seen.

I hadn't tried shopping in such a little town since I was a girl visiting Nana. I didn't remember that they rolled up the sidewalks so soon. It was only five o'clock on a Thursday night, but any store that looked like it might sell bedding was closed or closing. I drove up and down the Allenville downtown twice and then drove in ever-widening circles until I found a strip mall with a supermarket in it.

Unfortunately, it didn't have anything like a Bed, Bath, and Beyond, so I had to pull out into the street again.

A little farther down the road, I passed a sign for Wal-Mart and snorted. It would be a cold day in hell before Meg Taylor shopped at a Wal-Mart! Ever my mother's child, even when I was just scraping by as a graduate student, I had shunned the likes of J.C. Penny's for vintage shops.

It was her fault. She took me to the best children's stores, even when I was too little to care about what I was wearing. She took me to Macy's and turned her nose up at the likes of Sears and Mervyn's.

Once, I went to the mall with my friends and brought home a cute top from a teen-themed store.

"You must be joking," she said. She pinched the top and held it at arm's length.

"It's cute," I said. "And it was on sale."

"It's cheap. It looks cheap. It feels cheap. It makes you look cheap." She dropped the shirt back into the bag. "I didn't work my ass off in school and move away from the farm just so you could wear cheap, tarty clothes. We're taking it back."

And we did. She ground retail quality into me whether I wanted to learn or not.

I drove to the edge of town and back, searching for a name-brand store, any brand. I made yet another wide loop and, seeing no other options, found myself back in the Wal-Mart parking lot. Feeling my dignity drop down between my ankles, I turned my new car into the lot and parked it away from the beat-up pickups and ten-year-old sedans. Then I screwed up my courage and walked into the store.

I was a city-dweller, used to boutique shops containing only one kind of thing. At least, I was used to stores that contained lots of clothes, or food, or garden supplies, not all of the above. Wal-Mart was what would happen if Safeway had a love-child with Mervyn's. Wal-Mart was overwhelming.

Half of the building was tiled and shelved like a supermarket. Cool air wafted from the refrigerated sections and frozen food. Soft green light glowed from the produce aisle.

The other half was partially carpeted and signs overhead directed me to clothing, house wares, tools, and automotive. There was even a pharmacy. Wal-Mart was an entire town of shops under one roof.

I tried not to gawp like a hill person. I suppose I gawped like a city person instead.

I made my way to housewares by passing through the pharmacy and auto parts. I pulled down sheet sets and looked at thread counts and fiber content. It took a while before I found anything without any polyester, but the thread count was still just awful. I reminded myself that my own stuff would be arriving by truck soon and marched to the checkout.

I had to admit, things were cheap as hell. The sheets and pillows and comforter all together cost less than one fitted sheet from the set Martin and I had shared, which I burned in a trashcan in the backyard. By the way, make sure you burn things in a metal trashcan. Take my word for it.

I maneuvered my car through the empty streets of Allenville on my way home and marveled some more at how quiet it was. At 7:30 on a Thursday night, everything was open in Berkeley, not just bars and restaurants. I mean, I could buy a sweater, get a pedicure, and then have a late supper all after eight p.m. on a weeknight on Fourth Street.

The sidewalks in this town were vacant, and I found it weird that I could look into windows and not see people inside. Lights were off in the hardware store, the bookstore, the flower shop, the consignment shop. Even the cute little coffee shop was closed. I had a hard time imagining a place where coffee wasn't in demand after dinner. How many late-night coffee dates had I been on last year?

The one place that was still open was a sports bar and grill. There were cars in the parking lot and a group of people standing in the front door talking. I was briefly tempted to go in, but I had already hit a drive-through for a salad, and I told myself that I wasn't up for a night of being the new girl in town. But I did slow down a little as I passed to check it out.

The pod of people outside was backlit against the open door. They were laughing. It was an attractive bunch. The center of attention was a tall, sandy-haired man whose charisma captivated the group. He spoke, they laughed. For a moment, I was lonely enough to take my foot off of the gas and glance at the parking lot. But then a weary heaviness settled on me. I'd been there, done that. I was here to break the bar scene cycle, I told myself.

I drove away.

Once I was home, I made the bed, even though I hadn't washed the sheets—I forgot to buy laundry detergent. I decided that I didn't care about thread count as long as I had a warm place to lie down. Leaning against the kitchen counter, I ate my burger-chain salad out of its plastic clamshell. My TV was with the rest of my furniture on a truck somewhere south of here, so I flipped through a bodice-ripping romance novel. The heroine was flip-flopping between the rakishly handsome bad-boy and the steady, clean-shaven provider-type. I grew bored with her indecision and thought better about knitting without

TV to occupy the other part of my brain. I decided that what I needed was a bath. I filled up the tub with hot water and some shampoo for bubble and was already naked and dipping my toes in when I realized that I should have bought some towels, too.

I ended up drying off with my dirty clothes before I slid gratefully between the new sheets on my new bed in my new life.

Chapter 2

My friends didn't know what to make of me when I announced that I was moving to Oregon.

Beth shook her dark, $150 haircut at me and forbade me to leave the Bay Area. That didn't work, so she tried to convince me to settle in rural California instead.

"If you want land, I know they have some for sale in this state," she said over coffee when I broke the news to her.

"Oh, stop it," Margot had said, re-arranging a wisp of long, straight hair. "Meg is entitled to move away from the geographic center of her pain. I've been trying to get her to move out of that house since she threw Martin out."

"But *Oregon*?" Beth repeated. "Why not down the block? You know they have no good restaurants in Oregon, right? I read that in the *Guardian*."

"Listen," I said. "I'm not comfortable in that house. And I'm tired of living *here*."

Margot frowned. "But Berkeley is the most interesting city in the world!"

"And it's where *we* live!" cried Beth.

"I know," I said. "Look. I'm just tired of city life. I'm sick of the traffic. My place has been broken into once and my car twice."

"But you live in such a nice neighborhood," Beth said.

"Exactly." I wrapped my fingers around the warm ceramic cup. "I love you guys, but I'm really tired of all these other people."

Margot nodded sagely, sending flyaways haloing around her head. I knew what was coming. "Our Meg wants to go back to the land to look for inner peace," she said.

Beth leaned across the table. "I just can't see you shoveling shit," she whispered. "Isn't that why we went to graduate school? So that we could leave the shit jobs to someone else?"

"You're a snob," I said, repeating an old script. "But I'm not insane. This ranch comes with two on-site ranch hands that work for rent and a small salary. But I expect to get my hands dirty, too."

"All those summers on your Nana's farm are calling you, are they?" Margot said.

Beth blinked. "I thought you grew up in LA?"

"Sure I did. But I spent weeks in the summer at

Nana's farm in Gilroy. Plus, when I was a teenager, I worked at a stable in the city."

"I didn't know that about you!"

"I shoveled shit in exchange for riding lessons."

"So, why an alpaca farm and not a horse farm?" asked Margot.

I nudged a tomato to the edge of my salad. "I'm afraid of horses. Got kicked and broke my leg. You know, horses are really *big*." Then I smiled. "Alpacas are cute and fuzzy. Easy keepers. Remember?" I had bought two baby alpacas the summer Martin Left. They were now not so little and living happily on my Nana's farm.

"Cats are cute, too. And you could raise them here!" Beth said.

"I'm all for changing locations, honey," Margot said. "But a ranch in Oregon? That might be a bit excessive."

"I think I can do it," I said.

"By yourself?" asked Beth.

Dammit. There were those words. How many things had I ever done by myself? But this thing? This thing, I was going to do.

"Yes," I said. "By myself."

⌘

I had to admit "by myself" were two of my least favorite words. For most of my life, I took great pains to avoid saying them. I had a string of boyfriends in high school and college, one right after the other, because I hated the thought of going to a party by myself. Also, I always took Beth or Margot clothes shopping with me.

I know. Pathetic.

But that was the old me. Finding Martin in the shower with Nadja—"I'm from Sveee-den. Tch. You house so *dir-dy*"—changed all that, though it took some effort. I threw all his clothes out on the lawn and turned the sprinklers on. And the stuff he had left in the house after I got back from Nana's? Remember how I said to only burn stuff in a metal trashcan? Well, that was how I discovered plastic trashcans melt. Luckily, I had a fire extinguisher, but the yard stank for a week.

After that, I refused to speak to Martin, even on the phone. I didn't want an apology. I didn't want an excuse. I really didn't want an explanation. I wanted Martin and Nadja to evaporate. The image of his face and her naked ass pressed against the shower door needed to go away. I was convinced that wouldn't happen if I acknowledged Martin's existence.

My friends descended on my house during the divorce and formed a protective cocoon, armed with umbrella drinks and copies of *When Harry Met Sally* and *Pride and Prejudice*, but they had to return to their own lives eventually. I still had to crawl into my empty bed. From then on, I was "by myself." It made me think of Nana and how big and empty her bed must have felt after Poppy died.

My friends tried to help by fixing me up. Yes, I went on blind dates. Martin and I had been together for ten years. I was in no position to hit the bars, prowling for men. It took months of my friends pestering me, particularly Beth, before I relented. There was nothing like being betrayed by your spouse to taint your perspective on the opposite sex, and I wasn't in any hurry to be proved right in my suspicions.

Mostly, my friends set me up with nice, unexciting men who were all either obviously single for a reason, or recovering from relationship traumas as recent and painful as mine.

Sometimes I had a nice time, but I almost never hoped for a second date. I did once, though.

Margot set me up with Kevin, a tall, muscular man with a sunburn and a crooked smile. When I realized he was looking for me in the café, I felt a tickle of hope for the first time since I met Martin.

He smiled at me and I made a silent prayer to the dating gods.

We laughed about shitty spring weather and the slow service, and I felt so good. So comfortable. Kevin was normal, good-looking, easy to talk to, and sexy. He smiled at me and said charming things. I began hoping that I'd see him again.

But after our coffees arrived, things short-circuited.

"What do you do?" he asked. "Margot wouldn't say."

Wouldn't say? "I'm a securities advisor in the city."

"Really? You mean you schedule security for events and stuff?"

"No, the other kind of securities. Financial."

"Oh." His eyes got wider. "That sounds complicated."

"It's not too bad," I said. "I had a lot to learn at first, but I've been doing it for years."

"So, you, uh, went to school a long time for it?"

"Just an MBA," I said. "No more training than that, really."

"Wait, you have an MBA?"

"Yes," I said slowly. "Margot didn't mention that?"

"No." Kevin lowered his beautiful chiseled jaw to his chest and fiddled with his coffee spoon.

"So, where do you know Margot?" I asked. I hoped changing the subject would help.

"Margot orders products from my company for the grocery co-op she runs," he said. "She's a good customer."

"Which company?"

"All Earth Products," he said. But he didn't look up.

"I know that company. I like the products. My favorite is the lavender soap. Where do you get the lavender from?"

He made a small sound in his throat, like a laugh that got caught on bitter barbed wire. "I don't work that department."

I was losing him. I reached out and touched his arm. "Is there a problem, Kevin?"

After a long moment, he pulled back. "You're cute and sweet and funny…" he began.

"But?"

"But I'm—I only barely finished high school."

"And I'm over-educated."

"No, I'm under-educated."

"I don't care."

"I do." He looked at me, finally. "Me, I'm the shipping manager. Margot knows me because sometimes I drive the truck. I can't compete."

"I don't want you to compete," I said. Why was I so angry?

"You'll find someone who deserves you," Kevin said. He stood and kissed me on the forehead. Then he was gone.

I didn't cry until I was in my car.

დⴢⴢ

Unfortunately, after disheartening dates, I had to step inside my house where the silence was thick and the echoes smacked me around, reminding me of how very alone I was.

When dates went badly, my next strategy was cleaning, partly because I couldn't stand the thought of hiring a new housekeeper.

I found a new, sudden joy in scrubbing the grout between the kitchen tiles with a toothbrush. I began cleaning downstairs, sterilizing every surface and annihilating the dust bunnies in the living and dining rooms. Another night, I took on the stairs, wiping every curve on every banister spindle. I cleaned the bedrooms and even flipped the mattresses.

It took me a while to work up to it, but I finally attacked the master bathroom. I hadn't used it since that afternoon because the image of Nadja's lathered ass flashed whenever I glanced at the door. I even bought myself a new toothbrush and put it in the guest bathroom down the hall.

But I discovered the meaning of the word "cathartic" as I scrubbed the entire bathroom. It was horrifying because I kept imagining them as I had found them, all soaped up. I took frequent breaks to bawl my eyes out, sprawled flat on cold twelve-inch tiles. Eventually, I watched all the soapy scum of my life dissolve with the foamy cleanser and vanish down the drain.

And that's how I felt afterward: drained.

With the filth finally gone, the silence didn't bother me as much. I stopped fleeing my house. I begin knitting long, long, long scarves of alpaca wool. I spent more time with Margot and Beth, sipping coffee in the afternoons, not pounding shots of whiskey at night. I slept better.

But even though I felt better, I didn't feel the way I wanted to feel.

"I can't articulate it any better than that," I told Beth and Margot one chilly winter day.

"You just need to get back on the horse," Beth assured me. Margot rolled her eyes, but let her finish. "You'll find the right man, and all will be right with the world."

This was the same advice my mother gave me. I chose to ignore them both.

"You should come to laughing yoga with me," Margot said. "That will do the trick."

Sometimes I wondered how it could be that people who loved you had no idea who you were or what you were going through. My friends would do anything for me, but they didn't get me at all.

ⲉⲙⲉ

I awoke to a sharp rapping on my bedroom window. I pulled back the chintzy curtains—which I was changing as soon as possible—to find a dour-looking Molly standing in my flowerbed. She glared at me and pointed toward the front door. I pulled on a sweatshirt and met her there.

"Time for morning chores," she said. She looked at me from my bare feet to my flannel pajamas. "You wearing that?"

"Of course not." I yawned. She refused to come in, so I just shut the door while I pulled on my jeans and sneakers. As an afterthought, I pulled on a ball cap, too.

Molly harrumphed like an old man. "I suppose that'll do for today."

She stomped off toward the barn, so I followed, wondering what time it was. It was dark with a pale sliver of dawn cut up by naked tree branches. I could see Molly's silhouette against the lights in the barn as I stumbled after her.

Lew was already there, mucking out the stalls with alpacas milling around him like a sea of cotton balls. He smiled in greeting, but kept working. Molly shoved some black rubber dishes into my hands as soon as I stepped over the threshold.

"Half a scoop of pellets for each animal, dump it in

the troughs," she said and pointed at a galvanized garbage can standing in the corner. "I'll get the hay."

I looked at Lew, who was watching me with his now-familiar grin. I took the lid off the can and examined the pellets, which reminded me of the high-fiber cereal my dad used to eat, only green. I did my best to count the animals as they seethed behind the gates and scooped out what I guessed was the appropriate amount. Then I paused in front of the stalls.

Each pen had a series of troughs hanging on the gates, and all I had to do was reach over and dump the pellets in. However, all of the alpacas had shoved their heads over the rail, hydra-like, necks straining toward the pellets in the dishes I held. They jostled and reared and shoved each other like girls in the front row of a rock concert. I stood a moment, confused. How was I supposed to get to the troughs with this horde blocking me?

I glanced up and realized that Lew and Molly were wondering the same thing. Molly was peeking out from behind the stack of hay, but Lew was leaning on his rake handle, watching. I set my jaw. It was a test, was it? I always did well on tests. I looked again at the alpacas and saw a series of long, furry necks, puffy hairdos, and fuzzy lips. I realized that they were a bunch of cream puffs compared to the horses I used to groom. Plus, they were on the other side of the gate.

I took a deep breath and then stepped forward into the surge of eager noses. I pulled off my cap and whacked the nearest snout. "Get back!" I ordered.

The alpaca leapt backward as if a serpent had stung it

and blinked in surprise. I whacked another nose and another until all of the creatures were standing a respectful two feet back from the gate and I could pour the pellets unmolested. Once I moved away from the gate, they descended on the trough and gobbled the feed as if it was the last food on earth.

The alpacas in the other stalls had been watching and didn't need as much whacking to give me space. When I was done with the last pen of animals, I looked up to see that Molly was filling hay bins, pretending not to have seen anything, but Lew was still watching me.

He mouthed "Good job," before going back to scooping the poop.

I smiled.

By the time I was done in the barn with morning chores, I felt invigorated, but dirty. I peeled my clothes off, threw them in a pile, and jumped into the shower, using my pajamas to dry off with. Today, I needed to get some towels and figure out where my furniture was.

I stopped in the middle of my kitchen and thought of Old Mother Hubbard and her bare cupboard. I scooped up my car keys and headed into town for breakfast. Even though I had visions of a crusty bagel loaded with lox and capers, I found myself at a place that called itself The Pie House. It had good, bacon-scented fumes wafting from it and a parking lot full of pickups and SUVs. It also looked like the only sit-down breakfast place in town. I wondered if it was a place where the waitresses called you "hon."

It was.

"Just you today, hon?" my waitress asked.

Even though I hated that question, I just smiled, nodded, and sat in a booth. I sighed when I'd read the menu.
I'd lost the "I'm getting divorced" weight already, but
nothing on the menu here would help me keep it off. The
waitress returned, coffeepot and pad in hand.

"So, visiting?" she asked.

"Waffles," I said, answering the question I expected.
"Um, no. I just moved here." I tried not to blush as she
chuckled.

She poured the coffee and smiled. "Waffles. Where
from?"

I smiled back. "With fruit. California."

"Tch. Don't go telling everyone that," she said.
"There's lots who don't appreciate people moving from
down there, you know?"

"Really?"

She smiled and shrugged. "Silly, isn't it? Just say
you've come upstate," she advised. "I'll get you some
waffles."

The Pie House was trying not to be a greasy spoon. It
had been painted a dark plum color and the booths had
been re-covered recently. Still, in Berkeley, it would have
been a place students would have gone in the middle of
the night because Denny's was too up-scale. The clientele
didn't mind.

There were several booths filled with large men in
coveralls who didn't seem to need to be anywhere. The
oldest men had dirty ball caps sitting next to them on the
tables, while the younger—notice I didn't say *young*—

men kept their hats on. There were no other customers, certainly no one in a suit.

Even though I was sporting a sweatshirt and jeans, I felt out of place. Again. I realized I was biting my nails, but I couldn't stop myself. It kept me from crying, especially when the waitress messed up my order and brought me scrambled eggs and bacon, and they tasted just enough like Nana's to make me miss her, too.

As much as I missed Nana, though, that wasn't what kept me down. That was Martin. Or, rather, the shame spiral Martin had created.

Why had Martin cheated on me?

Why hadn't I been enough for him?

Why hadn't he loved me?

What had I done to deserve his desertion?

Why me?

I had lain awake many nights, obsessing about my divorce. I had decided that I was too fat, my hair was too curly, I hadn't been loving enough, I wore the wrong clothes, I served the wrong food at Christmas to his parents, I worked too much, or I hadn't worked enough. Dammit. I was sure the divorce was my fault, but I couldn't remember a single thing I'd done to cause it.

Last year, my therapist in Berkeley had talked me off this ledge a million times. I had her number on speed-dial, but today I was so exhausted that I couldn't call her. I couldn't re-live any part of last year, or last night, or this morning. I just had to move forward.

⌗⌗⌗

I realized last summer that I felt happiest when I was with my fuzzy little buddies at Nana's farm. I visited Nana frequently during my divorce, moping around the farm, petting the ponies I used to ride as a kid before the accident. One day, Nana led me by the elbow to her dilapidated pickup truck—the one Poppy had kept running with baling wire and spit. "We're taking a drive."

No one argued with Nana when she used declarative sentences.

We drove through miles and miles of flat Central Valley cropland, just greening up for spring. When we were kids and all the cousins piled on top of each other to go to a church picnic or the county fair, we'd play a crop identification game with Nana. She knew what each farmer was growing just by the few leaves poking through the soil.

"Corn!"

"Soybeans!"

"Beets!"

"Garlic!"

"Wheat!"

Nana would smile at the right answers and laugh at the wrong ones. The game got easier as the summer progressed, but I still found it devilishly difficult to tell a garlic plantation from one growing sunflowers—at least for the first few weeks of summer. Today, I wasn't even able to guess what the little leaves might turn into in a couple months. Eventually, Nana slowed her little pickup truck and pulled into the driveway marked by a sign that read *Ambrose Alpacas*.

"We're going to have lunch with Minnie Ambrose," Nana said.

"She doesn't have a thirty-something son living with her?" I asked.

Nana laughed. "No. Not at all. I think you need an alpaca adventure."

"A what?"

"Alpaca," Nana said, parking her pickup. "You know, little llamas."

I squinted out the windshield at what appeared to be a fuzzy white deer grazing in the field in front of us. It looked like the love child of a tribble and a giraffe. I followed Nana out of the car, confused.

"I've never seen one of these," I said.

"I know," Nana said. "My old friend Minnie sold her dairy a couple years back and bought a passel of these things. She loves them to death, and thinks she's won the lottery because she doesn't have to milk anything twice a day."

"And they make the most adorable sounds."

I spun around to see a tall, thin woman I recognized from summer church picnics.

She smiled. "Patty, Meg, if you'd a called, I would have brought the little ones in closer so we didn't have to hike."

Nana laughed. "I could use a walk. Let's go."

As we made our way through the paddocks, the alpacas followed us. They sniffed the air as we passed and stepped behind us until we passed through a gate. Then they clustered at the fence and watched us.

"They're curious about new people," Minnie said. "Although, to be honest, they follow me around the pastures, too." She laughed.

Finally, we arrived at a field with about ten adult alpaca and several tiny versions bouncing in the grass.

"This is the maternity pasture," Minnie said, holding the gate open for us. "Most of these crias are under two months old."

"Crias?" I asked.

"That's what we call a baby alpaca. It just means 'baby animal' in Spanish."

It looked like Nirvana. The grass was green. The trees were leafy and cool shade puddled under their branches. The alpaca moms grazed or dozed while the babies darted around their dams like an obstacle course. If their moms looked like fuzzy giraffes, the babies looked like they were made of pipe cleaners.

When we stepped in, one or two of the dams raised their heads and confirmed our benign nature, then returned to grazing. The babies bounced along as if we weren't there.

I felt the knot in my chest relax a little, for the first time in weeks, and took a deep breath. It felt like I had never had air in my lungs before.

"Sit down," Minnie said. "Enjoy."

I sat, instantly realizing that I had sat in something other than grass. "Eww."

"Oh, sorry about that," Minnie said, as concerned as she was amused. "You found one of their poop piles."

I was too embarrassed to speak, so I just moved to a

cleaner spot while Minnie and Nana talked about someone I didn't know.

I watched the shenanigans of the babies and smiled, even though my ass was wet, brown, and smelly. I didn't care. There was so much evident joy in that field, and I let it wash over me.

Then a brown baby noticed me. He strode over and stuck his little nose in my face. He blew warm, moist breath on my nose and gave my chin a whiskery nibble. I blew back as I would have with a horse, and he bounded off like an antelope fawn.

"Can I just fold him up and take him back to Berkeley with me?" I asked.

"No, but you can buy him and board him here until you get your own land," Minnie said.

"Or I can keep him at my place," Nana offered.

"Why don't you think about it, while your Nana and I go get us some lemonade?" Minnie asked. She and Nana walked, laughing, back to her house, leaving me cross-legged in the grass. I was surrounded by fuzzy, munching, humming, impossibly appealing creatures, and I didn't want to leave. Ever.

I decided I wanted two. "I'm paying for their vet bills and stuff," I insisted when Nana handed me a cold glass.

"Of course you are," she said. "But I'm taking the fiber to blend with the bunnies' fleece until you get your own farm."

"Deal," I said, smiling up at her. I wasn't looking forward to explaining this unexpected livestock purchase to my mother or my city friends, but Nana, Nana was one person who understood completely.

I drove down to see the alpacas more and more frequently, especially once they were weaned and moved to Nana's farm. I would sit in the pasture on a Saturday and read a book while they nibbled the grass or my shoelaces. I named them Seabiscuit and Secretariat because I'd just read those books, and I thought it was funny to name these fuzz balls after racehorses. I realized one day in that pasture as I watched Seabiscuit perform a Tigger-worthy bounce on Secretariat that I always felt more at peace on the farm than anywhere else in the world, and my little fuzz buddies made me feel even better.

So, a year after Martin and Nadja wrecked me, I began searching for the things I needed to build myself back up. I needed my own little piece of peace.

Chapter 3

I decided retail therapy would help my breakfast-induced homesickness some. I re-traced my steps to Salem, the state capital, twenty minutes from the Pie House. Funny how my GPS only began working once I was in a town that was big enough to support more than one Starbucks. It directed me along a highway over a river. Upon cresting the bridge, *Hallelujah*, a Nordstrom's sign greeted me. "I guess the state senators' wives need a place to buy shoes," I said to the GPS lady, who silently chided me for such a sexist remark. Before I could start actually arguing with the GPS that some senators might have male "wives," she informed me that I had arrived at my destination.

Ah, Nordstrom. It wasn't Saks Fifth Avenue, but I still emerged with bags stuffed with towels, excellent sheets, some cookware, and an electric kettle. Then I headed for a work-shoe shop. Of course, I had bought shoes at Nordstrom, but Lew said I needed something called a "muck boot." The saleslady actually sniffed when I suggested that the two-inch heels on the boots she showed me were impractical. The salesman pointed me at another store down the street that would have what I needed.

I should have put my shopping bags into the back of my car before entering the other shop. Not only was I the only woman present, I was certainly the only one with 100% Egyptian cotton towels bulging from my bags. A man in jeans and a hat ambled over to me, gave me an up-and-down glance, and smiled as if I was going to be a treat.

"Can I help you?" he drawled.

I sighed, instantly identifying him as an asshole. "I just need some muck boots."

"Oh? What for?" He didn't actually say, "little lady," but I heard it.

"My old ones are worn out, and I have to scoop poop tonight," I half-lied.

"Oh, well!" he said. "Right this way!" He led me to a wall, a literal *wall*, of boots. "What kind would you like?" he asked helpfully, calling my bluff.

"Um…actually, I hated my old boots. Find me something in an eight that won't hurt my feet or leak," I said, adapting my normal shoe-shopping technique. I just substituted "doesn't leak" for "looks cute."

He motioned for me to sit and then brought three boxes. I opened the first to see a pair of black, utilitarian boots made of rubber and neoprene. I pulled out the ugly boot and tried to look at it appraisingly. It looked exactly like the ones Molly wore. I sighed inwardly, reminding myself that they'd soon be covered in shit, and took the cardboard stuffing out of the toe.

"Here, let me help," the cowboy said, gently taking the boot from me.

I leaned over to unlace my sneaker, but before I could pull off the shoe, he plucked it off my foot. Then he cradled my heel just a moment too long before he slid the boot over my sock. "How's that feel?" he asked.

I didn't think he was talking about the boot. Before I could answer, though, he pulled it off and slid on another, trimmer boot, his long fingers wrapping around my instep between fittings.

"This one is a little more…dainty," he said, raising his eyes to mine. "For a daintier person."

I never thought I'd find a foot fetishist in a utilitarian shoe store. I imagined the types of feet he must usually see and shuddered inwardly.

I didn't get a chance to register an opinion about the "dainty" boot, either, because he slid it off and replaced it with a very, very cute red paisley rubber boot. I said, "Awww," before I could stop myself.

"I saved the best for last," he said, lowering my foot to the floor by sliding his hand all the way up my calf to the back of my knee.

"Okay," I squeaked, standing up. "I'll take it."

"Don't you want to try the other one on?" he asked in a slippery voice.

"Nope. I can tell this is the one. Plus…I'm double-parked."

I had to sit again to take off the boot and replace my shoes, making a big show of what a huge hurry I was in. I rushed to the checkout counter, clutching the boot-box, and thrust my credit card at the girl who stood behind the cash register popping her gum. She smiled at me in a way that seemed either cruelly delighted by my encounter, or jadedly sympathetic. She handed back my card. "Dave took care of ya, did he?"

"Um."

"Hate to say this, but you left all your shopping bags back there," she said after I signed the receipt. This time her smile was definitely cruel. Bitch.

ೲೲ

Later, I found the supermarket in Allenville, the town with the Wal-Mart, and went in search of some food and laundry detergent so I could wash my new linens. I didn't go to Wal-Mart for groceries because I decided that I needed rules about buying food and tools in the same store.

The supermarket was a soothing oasis of familiarity. Chain stores are coolly homogeneous on purpose, which is as good or bad as you make it. My father used to only eat at Denny's when he was traveling because he always knew exactly what he was getting when he ordered. He liked that predictability when he was on the road, away from home.

Why he ate at Denny's when he was at home, too, I'll never understand.

This store was almost exactly like the one in Berkeley I used to shop at, though the tea aisle was scaled down and the beer section had more domestics and fewer imports. Still, I knew exactly where to find the "healthy" frozen dinners and the laundry detergent. I was weirdly pleased by the efficiency of my market day, especially after the icky-ness of buying the boots. I was practically humming as I crept down the gravel road and turned up my driveway, even though I was still convinced that the slightest wrong move would send my car careening into the ditch.

Then, as I emerged from the trees, I could see a huge thing in my way. I slammed on the brakes, skidding, as, indeed, I knew I would, but not very far, considering how slowly I was going. Still, I was shaking when I stopped, and it took a minute to register what was blocking my path: it was an enormous truck.

"What the hell?" I asked the GPS lady.

When she didn't answer, I pulled the car over to one side of the driveway to see if there was some room to get by. As I squeaked past the truck, I cringed to hear the brush on the edge of the driveway scrape the side of my lovely new SUV. By the time I parked, I was so angry that I slammed the door and started looking for someone to shout at. Then I looked at the side of the truck. It was my furniture.

I should have been pleased, but I was pissed off because of the scratches in my car's paint and because no one had bothered to call me. The driver just shrugged and said he could come back next week if I preferred. I seriously doubted that was an option, but I took his point and let them into the house.

Molly and Lew came out of their trailer to help, which mostly involved them standing in the driveway and grinning as I panicked over the dents in the boxes and scratches on the furniture. The three movers seemed intent on increasing the number of dings and scratches as they practically tossed my things into my house as haphazardly as they could, heaping boxes in the wrong rooms and leaving dressers with the drawers facing the walls and the dining room table in a corner with the chairs stacked on top.

They were quick, though. Three hours later, the enormous truck was driving back down the driveway. I stood on the porch with Lew and Molly, watching it go. Then I turned and looked in the window at the living room. The formerly empty house, comforting in its sparseness, now looked as if a hoarder lived in it. There was only a narrow, crazy path from the garage to the kitchen, bordered on each side by leaning towers of boxes stacked atop my furniture. There wasn't even a spot to sit down.

I groaned.

Lew nudged me in the ribs with his elbow. "I suppose you only brought what you needed."

I had to laugh. I laughed so hard, I had to sit on the porch. When I could, I looked up to see that even Molly was grinning.

"What's in that big box?" she asked, pointing to one in the living room obviously labeled "bedroom."

"Shoes!" I dissolved into laughter again, as did Molly and Lew.

God love 'em, Lew and Molly spent the rest of the afternoon helping me shove boxes into the correct rooms. When there was a clear path through the house, I was at least able to open all the doors to the rooms.

"So, you hungry?" asked Lew.

"I could eat a bear," I said. "I mean, not literally."

Lew winked at me. "Well, come on over for supper."

"Really?" I looked at Molly, who was examining a pair of heels I had unpacked and actively not looking at me.

"Yes, really," Lew said. "We don't have any bear on the menu tonight, but I'm sure we can accommodate you, somehow."

"Um, if it's okay with Molly," I said.

Lew looked at his wife. "Whatcha say, honey?"

"Well, I did make an extra-big batch of stew."

"Great!" Lew threw an arm around my shoulders and one around Molly's waist. "I'll be disappointed if we can't find some bear for next time."

I wasn't sure I'd ever see the inside of Lew and Molly's place because she had been so cold the day before. Their singlewide was very, very old, and very, very pink on the outside. The tin siding had not been repainted in years, although it seemed to be holding up well. The wooden front porch had been replaced in recent memory, at least.

The inside was also a flashback to browner times. I wasn't a decorator myself, as my single-girl apartment used to announce to visitors. However, when I moved into said apartment, I tore down the old puce drapes and replaced them with some wispy things from IKEA. Molly and Lew had not.

Dominating the main room was a huge, brown, over-stuffed couch that had apparently grown out of the brown carpet. Flanking it were a pair of brass torchiere lights, and on the floor on the opposite side of the room sat a very large television. The wood-paneled walls were covered in pictures of families smiling down, many of the faces fading to orange with age.

The room smelled delicious, though. When Molly went into the kitchen and stirred a pot on the stove, I peeked over her shoulder at the bubbly brown heaven. I was inside-out hungry. "Oh my God, what is that?"

Molly smiled a little. "Best bison stew you'll ever have."

"I don't doubt it," I said. I left out the part that I had never knowingly eaten a bison.

Over the meaty, chewy, spicy meal, we talked alpacas, farm life, and backstories. I tried to tell them about Martin and Nadja without sounding bitter, but I wasn't sure I pulled it off. Both Lew and Molly looked sympathetic, at least.

"How about you two?" I asked, trying to change the subject before I went into too much detail. "When did you meet?"

Lew and Molly exchanged glances and smiled at

each other. "I was a widower," he began. "I finished raising our daughter myself and sent her out into the world. Then I was casting about, at loose ends, making a general pain of myself."

"We met at a country bar on Christmas Eve," Molly said.

"She was just standing there by herself—"

"I was with my sisters."

"So I introduced myself—"

"He grabbed my elbow and dragged me onto the dance floor."

"And the rest is history."

"He got my number and then hounded me until I agreed to go out with him again. And again."

She smiled warmly at Lew who tickled her chin. Molly giggled like she was six. It was the most unexpected sound I had ever heard.

"Well," I said, mostly to remind them that I was still there. "How long ago was that?"

"Oh, ten years now?" Lew stretched his long arms and then began packing tobacco from a pouch into his pipe. "Molly moved in with me soon after."

Molly shrugged. "I knew the people who lived here, so it was a no-brainer."

"I only know them from her signature on the deed," I said. "I've wondered why they sold such a perfect place."

Lew flicked open an eagle-emblazoned Zippo lighter and puffed on the fragrant tobacco a moment while Molly stared at the spot where the walls met the ceiling.

Eventually, he said, "It was a nasty divorce. Sounds

like a situation sorta like yours, only—"

"Only it was Sandra who cheated," Molly finished, her voice like battery acid. "Abe was oblivious until he answered his cell one day and the guy she was…with…spilled the beans."

"Why?"

"His sponsor told him to," Lew said. "A drunk. Frankly, so is Sandy."

"So, he called her husband and came clean? Then what?"

Molly shook her head. "Abe and I went to high school together. Sweet, sweet man. Didn't deserve that. He left."

"Moved," Lew said. "The judge made Sandy sell the ranch and split the profits."

"I see. Did she stay?"

"Moved to the coast with her drunk of a boyfriend," Molly said.

We sat for a while with these relationships swirling above our heads on Lew's scented pipe smoke. Lew's loss of his first wife and the betrayals of certain spouses hung in the air until Lew caught my eye. Then he squeezed Molly's knee under the table, and she squealed like a child again.

"I'm thirsty!" he announced. "Who's up for a beer?"

"After chores," Molly said. "Meg, never do chores drunk. Drunk people leave gates open."

"Fair enough," Lew said. "Let's see how fast we can get them done so we can get back here and get to drinking!"

It was only my third time doing barn chores, but I felt pretty confident. We three were beginning to move around like a team. I was in charge of measuring out and distributing the alpaca's pellets which, as Lew put it, were basically their Flintstone's vitamins: tasty and nutritious, but you wouldn't want to eat too many of them. Lew sorted the animals into stalls according to which feed they were getting, and Molly gave each stall its portion of hay. Then we all helped fill the water buckets at the hose outside the barn door.

When we were done, we stood a moment at the door, listening to the contented chewing of the animals as they tucked into their hay. A couple alpacas watched us with a wary eye, but most ignored us. Two stood at their gates, hay poking out of the corners of their mouths like stuffing from a scarecrow's sleeve, and waited expectantly.

Lew nudged me. "Watch this." He stepped forward and produced a baby carrot from a pocket. The animals' noses and eyes grew wider as he showed it to them and then held it in his teeth. The black alpaca blew loudly and stretched her neck out to him, snatching the treat from his lips with authority. The tan alpaca did the same.

"Your turn!" he said, pulling out another carrot and stuffing it in my hand.

I laughed. Soon I was standing with a carrot in my mouth, feeling fuzzy lips kiss mine. I had to giggle. "I love it here," I said.

"Good thing," Lew said, handing me another carrot.

ഉ∾ഉ

The good feeling wore off over the course of the weekend. I felt wonderful when I was outside with the animals, but when I was inside among the heaps and piles of my possessions towering over me, I became more and more depressed.

It really hit me Sunday night as I knitted another long scarf, cross-legged on the floor in front of my TV after eating yet another frozen dinner. I had spent the day unpacking clothes, shoes, and other things I'd need when I started work on Monday, but I had taken time to find my TV and at least get the digital equivalent of rabbit ears working so there were voices other than mine in my house. I could almost pretend that I had a friend over for dinner when I was unpacking if a game show was chatting in the background. Almost. I've never been that good at fooling myself—well, except when it came to Martin.

I sat surrounded by heaps of yarn and a scarf as I watched six—down from twelve—strangers try to kill a pig on a deserted island. I suddenly felt very small and alone. I ached for the guy on the show who was obviously going to be voted off the island. He let the pig slip through his grasp, and he knew he was done as soon as he heard the animal squeal in delight and beat a retreat to the other side of the island. He knelt in the underbrush, hollered a word that the network covered with a long, long beep, and then crumpled into what my yoga teacher used to call "child's pose," forehead to knees. However, I was pretty sure the sobbing and beating the ground he was doing was not part of the pose.

I wondered what I had done, which pig I had let slip

by, that made me deserve this loveless exile? Never mind that moving to the Oregon countryside was my idea. I still felt like the world had cast its ballot and thrown me into this lonely life where I knew no one except the people I paid to shovel shit. Even though Molly even seemed to like me now, I was still alone.

In order for a pity-fest to become a party, it needed more than one person. I picked up my cell and called Beth.

"Wow," she said when I finally paused for breath. "You sound lonely up there, Meg. Are you sure you don't want to come home?"

"No. Not yet," I said.

"But you've thought about it? We miss you."

"Way to twist the knife, Beth," I said, but I felt better knowing that at least she was thinking of me. "It's only been three days. I can't give up now. How stupid would I look?"

"Oh, please come home!"

"Not yet. I need to figure out how to do this first."

"If you say so," Beth said. "Shall I change the subject?"

"Oh, yes. Please."

"Well…" She launched into a two-hour description of her latest date and the maneuvers of Lily, her nemesis in office politics. I laughed at her outrageous stories. They were just what I needed to get enough perspective that I could go to bed.

છળછળ

Margot had understood when I finally refused to go on any more blind dates. Beth did not.

"I think focusing on the self for a period of time is good for the charkas," Margot said. She swirled her chai and then dipped in a whole-grain biscotti. "Get yourself re-balanced and you won't make the same mistakes you did last time."

"Oh, that's hogwash," Beth said, betraying her Midwestern roots. "You need to get out there and meet as many men as you can so you can find Mr. Right as soon as possible. He's not going to fall into your lap, you know."

I loved my friends, but they were a pair of hypocrites. Margot had been living with Peter for ten years, but neither of them wanted to get married. They even had occasional "side relationships" just to prove how unmarried and progressive they were. They were the most committed couple I knew, though.

Beth was more like me, flinging herself from one monogamous relationship to another in hopes of finding a real husband to walk her down the aisle. And though there had been a couple of catastrophic near misses, Beth remained a dark-haired romantic. But an unmarried, dark-haired romantic. I was now the jaded divorcée in the group.

"I'm just tired of the rat-race," I said. "I know Mr. Right isn't going to just walk in my front door and say, 'Here I am! Which side of the bed is mine?' But I want to get off the roller coaster for a while."

Beth shook her head, and I knew what was coming.

"You have to kiss forty frogs to meet a prince," she said.

I sighed. "I've kissed my forty," I said. "They are all still frogs."

"But now you're due for a prince!" she insisted, almost giddy.

"That's the kind of logic that keeps people at the slot machines," Margot said.

"Besides," I said. "I've never really been alone before. I'm kind of enjoying my time on my own."

I was lying through my teeth, but my friends kept their mouths shut, for once. They knew that it would only take a couple weeks before I was through my Netflix queue, and I had read everything I had always meant to read.

After a few weeks of not going out on dates, I started taking really thick books to the all-night coffee shop. I would carefully dress in shapeless sweaters, wear my glasses, and at least pretend to be absorbed in my reading, but, alas, it was Berkeley, and shapeless sweater plus glasses plus thick book were as much of a geeky-man magnet as tight dress plus too much eye shadow plus three-inch-heels were to arrogant assholes. At least the geeks were easier to rebuff than the men at bars were.

I wasn't committed to the moratorium on men until I finally realized that the restless itch inside that sometimes had me staring at my bedroom ceiling at night wasn't for lack of a man. Desperate for something to read, I had unearthed my aged copy of *My Friend Flicka* and took it to a coffee shop. Over a particularly good soy latte, I reacquainted myself with my all-time favorite book about my all-time favorite topics: people and animals. Then my thoughts went to my alpacas, Seabiscuit and Secretariat, hanging out on my Nana's farm, and I knew what I actually needed. I needed a farm, not a man.

And now, here I was on my farm, my own little piece of heaven. True, I was overwhelmed by homesickness, but I bounced in my seat like a giddy kid each time I drove through that copse of trees and saw my ranch from the driveway.

ၑၵၑၵ

It had only taken a couple phone calls to some friends in comfortably high places to land a position as a financial planner in the firm of Billings and Watt's in the little town of Hadley, Oregon. Hadley was big enough to have a place like the Pie House, but not large enough for the Wal-Mart, which was in Allenville up the road. Hadley was only a fifteen-minute commute from my house. And what a commute!

In the same amount of time that it took me to go two exits, while staring at the bumper in front of me in Bay Area traffic, I drove through little mountains covered in fir trees and stretches of green farmland dotted with the occasional flock of sheep or cattle.

I thought of Nana when I saw the sheep because she would care which breed they were, and I still couldn't tell one fuzzy white fluff ball from another.

I did recognize some cherry orchards, but they were in beginning to bloom, a sea of white popcorn strung on twigs, so the trees were easy to identify. The green crops in the fields, though, remained a mystery.

Billings and Watt's wasn't the kind of place I'd brag to my business school friends about working at, but they didn't have to know. Plus, I was only working there as a way to support the ranch until I figured out how to run that business well enough to do it full time. That was what I told myself, not my business school friends. I could imagine their eyes rolling now.

I found the address and parked across from the grand old building, a former bank built of brick in the Victorian age. On top of the arched windows and a real sense of presence, it even had a turreted tower on the corner. The building made me smile, which gave me hope as I marched through the front door and introduced myself to the pretty secretary stationed in the foyer.

"Ms. Taylor, yes. Please have a seat and Mr. Ridgefield, the manager, will be out in a moment."

I sat, crossing my ankles in my best impression of a ·confident, capable woman who was not actually consider- ing sitting on her hands to keep from gnawing on her nails.

I noticed the secretary was watching me as she an- nounced my presence on the phone.

"No, she's pretty cute," I overheard her whisper into the phone.

What the hell?

I didn't have time to make sense of this because, a moment later, a man in shirtsleeves and a tie rounded the corner with a grin on his handsome face and his hand thrust forward. "Ms. Taylor!" he cried as if we were long lost friends. "Good to finally meet you."

I stood quickly when I realized I had been staring at his chiseled face, sandy hair, and imposing physique. "Hello," I managed. "You must be Mr. Ridgefield."

"Please, call me Evan," he said.

He looked directly at me with blue eyes, which crinkled appealingly at the corners. I smiled and hoped I wasn't blushing. I willed myself not to drop my gaze coquettishly.

He stepped back a moment after he should have. "Follow me. I'll show you around."

As we passed the desk in the foyer, I noticed the secretary was watching us and had a peculiar, knowing smile on her face. A momentary wave of dread washed over me, and I wondered if Evan was a creepy foot-fetishist. Then I wiped that from my mind. Instead, I read her nameplate: Nancy Frost.

A little voice in my head whispered, *Watch out for Nancy Frost, Meg.*

The warning came and went, though, because my gaze traveled from Evan's broad shoulders down to the fine...cut...of his slacks. Those slacks made me reconsider my moratorium on men. What was it about cute, friendly men in the country?

I had always been a sucker for a fine pair of slacks, especially if they were fitted over a fine little ass and sat below a set of good shoulders. Evan's were at least as nice as Kevin the truck driver's had been. After we passed by a large room full of cubicles, Evan turned, smiled at me, and gestured to a little office with a door.

"This is all yours," he said.

I smiled back and waited for him to move out of the doorway, but he didn't step far enough to really make room. I had to slide by, doing my best not to brush against him. "Excuse me," I muttered.

Once I set my purse and bag down, I examined the room. It was big enough to turn around in, and that was all. The desk and two chairs about filled it. It was a third of the size of the office I'd had in Berkeley. "This is nice," I said, smiling. "A door and everything."

Evan had been watching me and still stood smiling in the doorway. "Great," he said, either ignorant of or entirely missing my sarcasm. "Want the grand tour?"

"Sure!" I was afraid I sounded too enthusiastic, but this time Evan stepped a little more outside the door so I could pass without actually touching him.

Once in the hallway, though, he put his fingertips on the small of my back, just above the waistband of my skirt. "This way," he said. "You'll want to meet the boss."

I was so shocked by his touch that I couldn't think what to do. I tried to ignore his fingers, but they made a little buzz on my back, and I kind of liked it.

The boss turned out to be a beautiful woman in her late forties named Penny Alverez. She smiled warmly at Evan when he walked into her office. She smiled when she saw me, too.

"Well, hello," she said, standing. "You must be Meg Taylor, our new personal finance assistant."

I shook her hand. "Ms. Alverez. I've heard a lot about you. Thank you for taking me on."

"Absolutely," she said. "You've got better credentials than anyone else on the team. How could we say no?"

I thought I caught her glancing at Evan, but I wasn't sure. I sat down in a chair that suddenly felt like a pincushion, and I tried not to squirm.

"Has Evan been showing you around?" she asked.

"Oh, yes," I said. "He's been a very good guide."

"I'll bet," she said as she picked up a file and handed it to me. "Here's a client to warm up on. Remember, though, you're not in an urban area, and these aren't urban people. Keep it simple."

"Yes, ma'am," I said. "Thank you again."

"Evan," Ms. Alverez said as we stood to go. "Stay here a minute, please."

I stood outside her closed office door, shifting from one foot to the other. Should I go back to my office, or wait for Evan? I could still smell his cologne—or was it just Zest soap?—hanging in the air, and I found myself imagining his morning routine.

I left when the voices in Ms. Alverez's office got louder. It seemed rude to stand there and half-listen to words I couldn't really understand. I dropped the file onto my desk and began arranging the few personal items I had brought: a plant I'd bought over the weekend, a sentimental coffee mug Beth gave me—of course, it was from Beth—and a grainy picture of the ranch I'd printed out from the realtor's website when I bought the place.

By the time I sat down behind my desk to open the file, Evan was back, his fair, lightly freckled face a little flushed. When he stepped into my office a dark shadow lifted from his features and he smiled at me. "Hiya. Want to get some lunch?"

I glanced at my watch. It wasn't even ten o'clock. "It's a little early for lunch," I said.

"Coffee? There's a place down the street. You must need a break—have a lot of questions." He seemed truly anxious, so I stood and reached for my purse.

We walked by Nancy Frost who raised an eyebrow at Evan. He waved her off. Weird.

"Is something wrong?" I asked outside.

"No, no, no, no, no," Evan said. He placed his hand on the small of my back again like it was the most natural place in the world for his fingers to be. I felt the buzzing again and stepped away.

Evan looked confused for a moment, but only for one moment. Then his smile flooded back. "Penny and I are working with a difficult client. I'd explain more, but confidentiality..." He led me down the street. "So, do you like it here so far?"

"I've only been here an hour, but so far I like it fine." I didn't like this urge I had to flirt with Evan, so I tried changing the subject. "Are all your clients rural?"

"Nah," he said. "Although, at this office, we don't get the huge accounts you must be used to." He glanced at me before continuing. "The biggest accounts are from the old families that own all the timber land. Those are the real whales around here."

"I thought there was no timber industry anymore. I read that somewhere."

"Nothing like before when I was a kid. But there is still lots of timber being cut. Only a few people own enough land to get rich anymore—or stay rich, rather."

"What do you mean?"

"Well," he said. "Have you noticed that the kids of rich people don't really pay attention to money?"

"I've seen a couple cases like that," I said slowly.

"Right." Evan must have seen something on my face. "That's all I mean. I've seen families lose money because the heirs didn't know anything about their finances."

I nodded. "It's sad when that happens."

"Well, here we are," he said, steering me into a warm little coffee shop.

We ordered drinks, but instead of going back to the office with our paper cups as I expected, Evan sat down at a table, so I joined him.

"Nice place. Come here often?" Dammit. He might think I was flirting. Evan was really cute, though.

He smiled, and I stopped berating myself long enough to admire his big white teeth. "Probably more often than I should." He looked around. "The place has atmosphere, doesn't it?"

Indeed, with all the tchotchkes and old movie posters on the walls, the café had more atmosphere than most places in Berkeley, which had recently been overrun with Starbucks clones.

"Yeah, I like it."

Evan leaned in closer. "The company is good, too."

I debated whether to smile back or storm out in a huff, raving about sexual harassment. I was used to being handled with kid gloves at work—I worked in the Bay Area, which was a hotbed for PC—so a big part of me was indignant at Evan's forwardness.

Another part of me was not indignant at all. That part of me smiled.

Still…

"Um. This is my first day."

Evan leaned back in his chair. "So it is," he said. "I should be showing you how to access your email and stuff, right?"

"Exactly," I said. I waved at the poster of Casablanca that hung over our table. "After all, we are at *work*."

ოჳ

I was feeling pretty good about myself as I parked in my new driveway. I was friends with Lew and Molly, the alpacas were wonderful, my first day of work was most satisfactory, and the sun had even decided to make an appearance on my drive home. Not bad.

The clients in the file Ms. Alverez had given me were straightforward enough: a typical family of "waited too long before we saved for retirement" who could be caught up in a few years with a slightly risky portfolio. Well, they were "typical," except that their major source of income was a hazelnut orchard.

And, of course, there was Evan. Even though I was a dishwater blonde with a curly bob, I had never been attracted to redheads. But I had *always* been attracted to broad shoulders and cute little tushies. Evan's torso more than made up for the aversion to freckles I had harbored since junior high school.

Plus, Evan was obviously interested. I had to admit, it was nice to feel desired. It made me wonder, though. Did he hit on every woman who stepped in the door like that?

I opened my car door and almost knocked over a panting Lew. "What is it?"

"Got a call in to the vet, Miss—Meg," he said. "One of the dams got caught in the fence."

I followed his pointing finger to where Molly knelt in the field next to a still black form. "Oh my God!" I cried. "Will she be all right?"

"Don't know," he said, looking beyond me. "Here's the vet. Let's go." He strode over to where the vet's pickup truck had rolled to a stop behind me.

"Oh, shit, oh, shit, oh, shit!" I leapt from my car and ran into the house, ripping off my skirt and pulling jeans on over my panty hose. I stuck my feet into my new red boots and sprinted to the vet's truck still in my good blouse and office jewelry. "What's up, doc?" I said and then groaned. I hadn't meant to be funny.

Lew didn't help by grinning a little. "Cody? You remember Meg."

Dr. Arden shook my hand once before turning back to his supplies. "Glad to see you again," he said to a sack of gauze and tape.

He was tall and lanky with a handsome face that had

seen too much sun. His curly dark hair was in serious need of a trim so it didn't fall in his eyes so charmingly as often.

"Let's go," Dr. Arden said, handing Lew a bucket and me a box of first aid supplies.

I trotted after the two men who climbed through the fence one-handed. I had to put my supplies down to get through the wires, but no one seemed to notice. I decided not to be embarrassed and hurried down to where the injured animal lay.

"So, tell me what happened," I asked Lew, when I caught up to them.

"Missy likes to rub on the fences—scratching. We think she got one foot between two wires and then the rest of her fell through. She's been out there maybe an hour, maybe all day."

"Can she stand?" Dr. Arden asked.

His voice was so even and calm that I looked at him. Even happy-go-lucky Lew was really concerned, but Dr. Arden sounded like he was getting ready to transplant a fruit tree.

"Hasn't tried, but we wouldn't let her, anyway."

"Is she free from the wire?"

"Yeah," Lew rubbed his head. "It took some doing, but we were able to loosen the fence and get her foot out."

"Why didn't you call me?" I asked him.

Lew shrugged. "Your office said you were already on your way home, so we called the vet instead."

We arrived at where Molly knelt on Missy's shoul-

ders to keep her from trying to stand and rubbed the alpaca's black ears. Molly cooed reassuringly and was
making a point not to look at the ragged mess of red and
white on the alpaca's back leg.

"Oh, God. Is that, that bone?" I asked, the world tip-
ping a little.

Dr. Arden knelt next to the animal. "Yep."

Then I found myself sitting on the wet ground, feeling light-headed. I looked up to see Lew and the vet
kneeling next to me.

"You okay?" Dr. Arden asked, one hand on my
shoulder, the fingertips of the other hand on my chin,
turning my head and peering into my eyes.

His eyes were large and brown with dark lashes
brushing his unkempt eyebrows.

"I'm just—there's bone—is she going to be okay? I
saw a horse caught in a fence die," I said.

Dr. Arden smiled at me and cupped my cheek with
his palm. "No, she'll be okay. Alpacas are smarter than
horses and will lie still if they're trapped. I don't think
this is a bad wound. We'll get her fixed up." Gently, he
took the box of supplies from my hands and stood. "If
you feel faint again, put your head between your knees."

I nodded and breathed slowly for a while. I watched
the three of them work on Missy. Dr. Arden deftly
cleaned, trimmed, and stitched the wound as I watched,
woozy but fascinated.

Within a few minutes, Missy was standing on her
newly-stitched leg humming loudly to the rest of the
herd, which had taken refuge from the vet at the far end

of the pasture. Dr. Arden knelt next to her, explaining to Lew and Molly how to change the dressing, when I stepped up behind them.

He looked over at me and smiled. "The bone is covered up."

"Thanks," I said. "Can I help?"

"Really?" he asked.

I saw Lew and Molly exchange a glance, which firmed my resolve.

"Yes," I said as I dropped to my knees beside him. "I want to learn."

"Okay," the vet said, brushing his hair out of his eyes. "I was telling them that you'll need to go buy a box of disposable diapers. Best bandages for this kind of thing."

Shoulder to shoulder, he helped me slather on an antibacterial goo and then cover it with gauze and a type of stretchy bandage—vet wrap—I remembered from the stable long ago.

"This needs to be changed once a day for at least a week. Can you do that?"

I looked up from smoothing out the bandage on Missy's leg to find him watching my face. I smiled and scratched my cheek. "I think I can handle this if someone holds her," I said. Then I looked down at my sleeve where I had just wiped a dark brown smear of medicinal goop. "Oh, my silk shirt!" I cried. I jumped up and ran back to the house. Then I remembered my manners, turned back, and called, "Thank you!"

Molly was grinning, Dr. Arden was chuckling, and

Lew was laughing. Mortified, I fled to my bathroom and locked the door, as if they might follow.

The mirror wasn't kind. The smudge on my blouse was what clued me in, but I was not prepared for how I looked. The brown goo was streaked across my cheek, which was why it itched. My hair was wild and boinging in all directions, and there was a huge wet spot on my ass where I had landed in the pasture after fainting like a wimp.

Still worse, the vet was cute and kind. What must he think of someone who goes into a field in jeans, red paisley boots, and a silk blouse, and who faints at the sight of bone? The man who took care of my animals must have thought I was a scatter-brained wimp.

I sighed. The blouse was a lost cause. Aside from the goo, I'd managed to get the elbows muddy—I hoped it was mud—when I'd fainted in the field. I tossed it in a corner of my bedroom beside a box labeled *Garage*, and pulled on a tee shirt and my last clean jeans. I found a ball cap and headed for my car. I was in need of some warm, non-frozen dinner and a box of diapers.

Chapter 4

After some of the worst Chinese food I'd ever eaten—*note to self: never eat at an Asian restaurant where all of the vehicles parked outside are large pickups*—I made my way back to the supermarket I'd found earlier. Soon, I was standing, befuddled, in front of a huge aisle of diapers. Who knew there were so many kinds of diapers? I mean, I expected there to be different sizes, but what the hell was a "natural" disposable diaper? Weren't all disposable diapers designed to last until the end of days? I wondered what "Little Movers" had over "Crawling Ease." And what did mommies do if they didn't choose the "overnight" diapers? Wake up Junior halfway through the night to change him?

I was so absorbed that I didn't even notice the thin little woman in jeans and worn boots next to me until she spoke.

"How old?"

"What?"

"How old is your baby?" she asked.

I blinked for a moment. No one in the city would ever dream of talking to a stranger in a supermarket, much less inquire after her kids. Then something more horrifying occurred to me: She thought I was somebody's mommy! How far had I let myself go? I tried to smooth my sweatshirt as I said, "I don't have a baby."

"Oh? Whose baby are you buying for?" the woman persisted, no apology or anything.

"Not a baby, an alpaca," I said, lifting my chin.

"An alpaca? Well, I think you should go for the biggest size, then." She handed me a package of jumbo-sized diapers.

I had to laugh. "Oh. I need these to bandage her leg. Not for her to wear."

"Oh, good." The woman laughed. "I was trying to imagine why—some people do weird things with animals, you know?" She put the huge diapers back and handed me a much more modest-sized package. "I'd probably cut these in half, even," she suggested. "I'm Rosie," she said, extending her calloused hand to shake mine. She had a long red braid down her back. "I have a little horse ranch south of town. Where are your alpacas?"

"Just west of town," I said. "Thanks."

"Sure thing," Rosie said. "Here's my card. If you need anything, let me know. It's tough getting started ranching."

"How did you know I'm new at this?" I asked. "Do I have a 'Greenhorn' sticker on my forehead?"

Rosie grinned in a familiar way. "I knew the family that owned your ranch. I heard from Sandy that you were moving up from Berkeley. Plus," Her grin grew even more familiar. "Lew's my dad."

"Ah ha," I said. "Then you'll hear a good story about how I impressed the vet this afternoon."

"Dr. Arden?"

"Yeah." I could feel myself blushing. Again. Some more.

"He's a cutie-patootie," Rosie agreed. "What'd you do? Fall in the poop pile?"

"Basically."

Rosie laughed. "Listen, the last time he saw me, I was covered in you-don't-want-to-know, and I was still in my pajamas."

"I just felt like a fool," I said. "It's not like I need to impress anyone, but I hate feeling like, like…"

"Like you don't know what you're doing," Rosie finished.

I nodded. "Like I need help."

She patted my shoulder. "I get it. I'm like that, too. If you have questions," she said, "don't be afraid to call me. I won't tell."

I waved as she rounded the corner and then tucked the card into my wallet. I had a feeling I was going to need it.

❧❧

A long shower helped me feel more like myself and less like a poser city-chick in the country. I stood at the counter, mostly because it was the only clear horizontal surface in my house, to nibble on some popcorn. I couldn't see the TV from there, so I flipped through what passed as a local newspaper. The *Editor-Picayune* didn't bother with an international or even a national news section. It was all local news with little columns for each of the teeny communities in the area, documenting everything from weddings to people's tropical vacations and high school dances. I had no idea that newspapers like that still existed. It read like a historical document.

When it was dark, I slid between my Nordstrom sheets and tried to settle into my spy-thriller novel, but my mind kept drifting between the handsome, forward man at work to the quiet, competent man in the field. Every time the author indulged in a little exposition, either Evan or Cody would insert himself into the scene, picking up a clue or just standing in the shadows. Finally, I slammed the book shut. One fucking day at work and alone for the first time in my life, and suddenly it's raining men.

"Way to go for a new beginning, Meg," I said. "Why don't you just find a womanizing jackass like Martin and get the heartbreak over with as soon as possible?"

I punched my pillow until my arm hurt and I felt better. I went to sleep, angry with the male world.

However, my unconscious mind had a different agenda. My first dream was of my high school boyfriend. Our prom picture had been picked for the local newspaper. We cut out the page and then fell to necking.

Then I was with Bobby, and we were on the beach in Cabo, sipping umbrella drinks on the sand, like Mr. and Mrs. Clyde of Perrydale. We didn't go anywhere together in real life except to his mom's house one Thanksgiving.

Finally, the highlight reel from my relationship with Martin flitted by in grainy Super-8: expensive dinners, trips to the Bahamas, his proposal in New York City in the springtime, our wedding. His crinkly smile and dancing hazel eyes made me smile, and I awoke in the black country night feeling so warm and happy that I reached across the bed, only to find cold emptiness.

ო჻ო

I was nearly late to work because Missy's bandage took more time to change than I'd bargained for, but I'd discovered a drive-through coffee stand the day before and took the chance that they sold muffins as well as caffeine. They did.

There was a small vase of flowers and note on my desk when I arrived that morning. I set my vanilla soy latte down and tossed the muffin beside it before I picked up the note card.

Welcome to Billings and Watt's! it read. The line beneath it said, *Please come to a welcome dinner tonight at River's Restaurant at 5:30.*

Taking a new associate out to meet the company personnel was a really nice gesture. I plugged the dinner into my very, very blank calendar.

I smiled and looked up to discover Evan in my doorway.

"Like the flowers?" he asked.

"It's a sweet gesture," I said. "Do you do this for all the new employees or just the associates?"

"I don't give just anyone flowers," he said.

"Oh, these are from you?"

"Yes. No, I mean, I ordered them, but it's the company's ticket," he said. "Are you coming tonight?"

"Sure thing."

"How about the after-party?" he asked.

I turned the card over. "There's nothing here about an after-party."

"I'm joking." Evan laughed. "The people who work here aren't exactly the after-party types, you know?"

"I suppose not. Most of the people I've met so far look more like they need to get home to feed the kids."

He smiled, sitting in my client chair. "Especially on a Tuesday," he said. "Nothing like us young singles, huh?"

I shrugged. "I don't usually go out on weeknights, especially not after the divorce." I was quiet a moment, letting that bit of information sink in. Then I changed the subject. "There was this one place down on the boulevard that had two for one margaritas on Tuesday nights, though."

"Indeed?" Evan sat back and put his hands behind his head, showing off his deep chest and flat abs to great effect. "That sounds like a place for an after-party."

I shook my head. "Honestly, I got so sick of the bar scene…"

"So sick of it that…"

I turned and fiddled with my computer. "I gave it up."

"You gave up two for one margaritas? What happened?"

I shook my head once and typed in my password for my email. "Men are stupid beasts," I heard myself saying. I glanced at him.

He sat up in his chair and put his hands on his knees. "So, no more city dating, huh?"

"Nope."

"You know, the men up here are different," he said.

Was the look in his blue eyes actually sincere?

"Perhaps," I said. "They certainly can't be any worse." Even I was surprised at the bitterness in my own voice.

"Don't worry, they are," Evan said, standing. "Different, I mean. Better. Not worse."

I had to laugh with him as he stepped out of my door. The words "What a sweetie" tumbled from my lips before I knew it, and I had to shake my head to regain my perspective. Martin had been a sweetie, too, until he'd taken a long shower with a short tart.

꿍

Six or seven people were at the steakhouse when Evan and I arrived. He dropped by my office just as I was packing my things up and insisted on driving both of us there since he knew the way. I only hesitated an instant. I hate to admit it, but I caught a whiff of his soap, broke into a smile, and said yes.

The restaurant was small and charming, built into a historic narrow brick building along the town's small riverfront. Sounds of clinking glasses and early dinner chatter bounced pleasantly off the walls. When they saw us enter, a welcoming cheer arose from my new office mates, and I blushed a little. Then Evan's fingers were on my spine again, directing me to join the group.

"Ms. Alverez," I said right away. "Thank you so much for this."

"I'm Penny outside the office," she answered. "We try to make new people feel welcome." She handed me a glass of wine. "Drink up," she said with a peculiar smile. "The free drinks at the welcome dinner are one of the few perks of working here."

The pinot noir was good, better than most of the stuff from Southern California, actually. The food was good. Even the company was good. In fact, my co-workers were quite an interesting bunch once they started drinking a little.

As I had guessed earlier, most of them were married with kids, but I was surprised by how much fun they were. My friends with kids in Berkeley constantly fretted about earth-friendly diapers, which pre-schools to pre-enroll in, and high-fructose corn syrup. They carried anti-bacterial wipes and little bottles of Purell in their designer purses and threw away anything that touched the ground, ten-second rule be damned.

Not these people. They were happily showing off

pictures of their kids swimming in lakes, drinking from garden hoses, riding horses while eating apples, and making mud pies.

They even talked about kids' movies without the sniffing disdain I was used to.

One couple, Danielle and Ross, welcomed me with another glass of wine. "Sometime, you have to come taste some of our wine," Ross said.

"You make wine?"

"From our own grapes." Ross swirled his glass and critically watched the wine spin. "It's not as nice as this, but not bad for a half-acre amateur."

Danielle shook her head. "I bought him a vine ten years ago because I thought it would look nice on our pagoda. Now he's obsessed. He's even got the kids in the vintner course through 4-H."

"At least you've got some nice wine out of it," I said.

She nodded. "I am the beneficiary of all his experiments. Good and bad."

"Oh, the 2008 wasn't that bad a vintage," Ross said.

"We used most of it to kill weeds," she staged-whispered.

They both laughed. They showed me pictures of their kids stomping grapes with their bare feet in a kiddie pool.

Evan was very attentive, always making sure everyone's glasses were full—especially mine. Before I knew it, it was eight o'clock and people were beginning to file out, laughing and full of good cheer.

When Evan trotted out to pull the car around, I felt a light hand on my elbow. I turned to find pretty Nancy

Frost behind me, smiling primly. "Mr. Ridgefield certainly has taken a shine to you," she said.

"I suppose he has," I said.

I was warm enough with wine and food that I was pleased someone else was confirming Evan's attentions. No thought of the evils of men had crossed my mind since pinot noir number two.

"Meg." Nancy's hand returned to my arm. "It's none of my business, but be careful." She jerked her head slightly over her shoulder.

I followed her gesture to see Penny taking care of the bill with a company credit card. My boss looked up at me, so I waved a little and then looked past her to where Evan stood at the door beckoning to me.

"Uh, thanks," I said to Nancy. "Gotta go."

I had to pass Penny on my way to the door, so I stopped to thank her again.

"Of course," Penny said. "You're only new here once, you know."

I felt my boss's eyes on me as I walked out the door with Evan. "What were you talking to Nancy about?" he asked as he opened the car door for me.

"Hmm? Oh, nothing," I lied. "She was just giving me some tips about working for Penny—Ms. Alverez."

Evan slid behind the steering wheel and started the car before he peeked at me from the corner of his eye. "So, where to?" he asked.

"What do you mean? My car's still at work."

"It's kind of early," he said. "There was talk of an after-party."

"So there was," I said. My mind whirred a little. I smiled. A handsome man wanted to extend the evening with me. "I'm probably too silly with wine to drive home right away, anyway."

"I know this little place—" Evan began. "Good drinks, private, close by—"

"As long as it isn't your place, it sounds great."

"Awww." Evan whacked the steering wheel with his palms. "But I have streaming video. We could watch anything."

That's a dumb idea, my brain said. *This guy wants to get into your panty hose.*

Wait! another part of me said. *Maybe it's time to take off the panty hose. It's been a really long time, you know.*

My mouth said, "I haven't seen *My Friend Flicka* in a long time."

"Done," he cried and made a series of quick turns that my addled brain couldn't follow.

Though the outside of his house was just like the other cookie-cutter houses on his block, the interior transcended the bachelor-pad pastiche. I inwardly cringed when I compared it to the Nuevo-cardboard-box theme at my place.

"Nice," I said. "Who's your decorator?"

Evan shrugged out of his coat. "Ex-wife," he admitted.

"Ah ha. My ex left an assortment of mismatched socks and took my grandfather's watch. I think you came out better than me."

Evan rolled his eyes. "Let's not talk about the exes,"

he said, opening yet another bottle of wine and filling two glasses. "Let's just sit. And drink."

I took my glass, sat on the couch, and sipped my wine. "This isn't going to help me sober up enough to drive home."

"Hope not," Evan muttered, sitting next to me.

I set my glass down on the coffee table and put a finger on Evan's chin. "Listen to me. I am going to go home tonight."

"Okay," he said. "Are you going to do anything else?"

I raised my eyebrows and tapped his nose. "Maybe."

"Good enough for me," he said.

He took me into his arms and kissed me. It had been months since I had been part of a good snogging session, and Evan did not disappoint. He kissed with great variety: gentle nibbling, lower-lip suckling, and neck tickling from my earlobes to my collarbone. For my part, I kissed all his freckles, paying special attention to the ones I found behind his ears. We laughed a lot and forgot to drink the rest of the wine.

But, with great effort, I managed to keep my clothes on and peel myself away from Evan around eleven. He drove me back to the office and pulled up next to my car.

As I opened the door, he caught my arm. "When can I see you again?" He was sad-eyed, his hair was tousled, and he looked good enough to eat.

"Tomorrow morning."

"No." He laughed and kissed my palm. "Alone."

"Friday?"

"That's days away!"

"Come on," I said, pulling my hand away. "We need to make up for the trashy office-party hook-up with something a little more classy, don't you think?"

"Fair enough," he said.

I closed the door and then leaned in the window for a kiss. "I definitely want to do this again," I whispered, and then I went to my car.

I was surprisingly sober, and I fairly flew home, not even thinking about the dark, skittery gravel road. Instead, I thought about Evan and his warm skin, playful smile, and soft couch. My head was so full of Evan-ness that I almost missed the note taped to my door.

Meg,
Please call us if you are going to miss evening chores. It is easier to do them before sunset than in the dark.
Thanks. Molly and Lew.

"Shit." I felt about two inches tall as I crept into my house like a teenager caught breaking curfew. As my head hit the pillow, another thought occurred to me. I still had to get up at six a.m. to dress Missy's leg wound. I groaned when I realized that I was probably going to have a hangover, too.

I dragged my ass out of bed and took my college roommate's patented hangover cure: three Ibuprofen, a multivitamin, and a pint of water.

When I crawled back into bed, I remembered another

reason I'd stopped dating. For all the fun evenings, the mornings after were hell.

☙☙☙

The next morning greeted me with a shaft of sunlight directly in my face, which did not make my headache any better. My roommate's hangover cure was no better than her multiple-choice test strategy where she just filled in the bubbles to spell ACDC over and over again.

I swatted at my alarm, which was reminding me that it was after six a.m. I was already running late.

I appeared in the barn, squinty, but dressed. Lew and Molly were hard at work, Lew with his signature grin and Molly indignantly ignoring me.

"Sorry about last night," I said, gathering the diaper and goo and stumbling to Missy's stall.

"Must of been important," Molly said.

"No," I said as I caught Missy. "It was a welcome dinner."

"Aw, that's nice," Lew said. He came over to hold the alpaca for me. "We wouldn't expect you to miss something like that. Would we?" he asked Molly.

Molly pouted a little. "Just give us a heads-up so we know to start without you."

"Of course," I said. "If I'd been thinking, I would have."

Lew cradled Missy's long neck so she would stand still while I pulled on my latex gloves and began unwrapping the vet wrap.

I peeled the diaper from the leg and examined the wound.

"How's it look?" Lew asked.

I took some gauze from my kit and wiped the wounds, stopping when Missy flinched. "Better, I think," I said.

Honestly, my head was pounding so much I couldn't see straight, but the edges of the wound didn't look as angry as the day before. I applied new salve and a fresh diaper/bandage and wrapped the whole thing with new red wrap. I sat back and admired my work.

"Cody would be proud," Lew said.

It took me a moment. "Oh! Dr. Arden. Cody. You think he'd approve?" I smiled as I stood.

"Sure." Lew patted the alpaca and sent her on her way. As he held the stall door open for me he said, "I hear you've also met Rosie."

"Hmm? Oh, at the supermarket. She helped me get the right diapers."

"Apple of my eye!" he said. "She's a wealth of information. You should see her place."

"Sounds like fun."

He smiled in a way that made me look at him again. "What?"

"Nothing," he said. "Knows everyone in town. Like Cody. That's all."

"Weirdo," I said without thinking. Fortunately, Lew guffawed and Molly had to sit down from laughing so hard. "You're both weirdoes," I said. My head felt lots better.

I patted another alpaca's back. Her head was plunged into the hay bin, so she didn't even look up at me. She was too busy eating.

"Who is this again?" I asked.

"Angela," Molly said. "She's convinced the best hay is at the bottom of the bin."

I smiled. "It seems to be working. She's really fat."

"She's due in a couple weeks."

"You mean like pregnant?" I asked.

"No, she means like for a dentist's appointment," Lew said.

I almost said, "Really?" but I saw the look in his eye and just grinned instead.

Angela used her head to flip the bin over and spread the hay over the ground, looking for that perfect mouthful.

"I don't know why I even bother putting in clean hay," Molly grumbled. "They eat off of the ground outside, anyway." Then she set bins of hay into the other stalls.

I knew better than to laugh at her, but Lew didn't and had to duck when she threw her gloves at him.

ⓔⓢⓔⓢ

With the help of the drive-thru coffee shack and its muffins, I wasn't technically late for work, though it seemed that everyone else in the office had arrived on time and was positively chipper. I tried to convince myself that I was just paranoid when it seemed that everyone, especially Nancy and Penny, could see how hungover I was, and that everyone else was wildly speculating where Evan and I had gone after the party. My car had been in the office parking lot until eleven, after all.

What a tramp! Two days on the job, and I'd already gone home with the office hottie. I felt even more nauseous.

Evan looked exactly as ragged as I felt and only managed a sheepish wave as he passed by my door. What a creep, I thought. Wrecking my good reputation before I even had a chance to build it up. I glared at my computer as my head pounded. How dare he take advantage of me when I was drunk. Well, a little tipsy, anyway. How dare he make me feel good about myself and, and...

I was too tired to be mad, so I put my head on my desk.

A little later, as I walked past his door to get even more coffee, I saw him behind his desk, head in his hands. I knew the position well. The rational went something like this: "If I keep squeezing, either my head will squish, or the pain will stop. I have no preference." I felt sorry for him.

"Do you want some aspirin?" I asked on my way back to my desk.

"Already got a handful," he said, not looking up. "But thanks." He peeked up at me and managed a smile. "I'll be by later when the world stops shouting at me."

When he did turn up in my doorway an hour later, I welcomed him with a smile. But before either of us had a chance to say anything, my phone rang.

"Meg?" Penny's voice was curt. "Is Evan there? Tell him I need to see him, now."

I stared at the receiver for a moment. I hadn't said anything at all before Penny hung up. "Penny wants to see you—now," I told Evan.

He frowned. "What for?" he muttered as he turned and left.

I didn't know why, but I was suddenly nervous. I stared at the open file on my desk without reading it and then doodled on the margins of my notepad. It was like one of my friends had been caught at a party neither of us was supposed to be at. He was in the principal's office for something we both did. Was it my turn next?

I nearly leapt from my seat when a very grumpy Evan reappeared. "I'm supposed to go to Seattle to the main office for training."

"Oh," I tried to conceal my relief. Of what, I wasn't sure. "When do you leave?"

"Today."

"Oh. And you'll be back?"

"Friday night. Late." He looked sorry. "Can we re-schedule our 'real date'?"

"Of course."

"Saturday?"

"Yes." I smiled, but then squinted at him carefully. "You look like I feel," I said finally.

He laughed. "I just hope I feel as good as you look soon."

As soon as he was gone, the phone rang, and Penny summoned me into her office, as well. By the time I got there, I was picking the nail polish off of my right thumbnail.

"Ms. Taylor," she said. "You look…unwell."

"It's my own fault," I said, deciding that lying about a hangover would make things worse. "I don't drink red wine much, and I lost track of how much I had last night." While both statements were true, I decided to omit the part about choosing a necking session with a co-worker over a reasonable bedtime on a work night.

Something told me that I wasn't fooling Penny. However, despite her narrowed eyes and tacked-on smile, she chose to accept my explanation. "I have some new clients for you," she said, sliding a pile of files toward me. "They're a bit more…challenging…than the people we started you off with. Good luck!" she sang as a dismissal.

I took the stack back to my office. I was staring at the pile, wondering where to start, when Nancy stepped through my door.

"Oh, my," she said, stopping short. She was holding huge stack of file folders. "So that's where all the problem files went. Usually, I divide them up three or four per associate." She gave me a sympathetic look. "Penny gave these all to you?"

"Yeah." I opened a file on top and glanced at it. It was a mess, but it wasn't too bad. "They're all like this?" I asked.

"Afraid so," she replied, setting down the stack she'd brought. "She had me bring these over, too. Let me walk you through a few of them."

"Thanks."

"So, these all got corrupted the last time we changed computer systems," she said. "It's grunt work, but the penciled amounts need to be re-entered into the system."

I caught her eye. "Why do you think…"

"Why'd Penny give these all to you? I can't say for sure," she said. "But she's had her eye on Evan since the day he walked in here."

"But, he was married."

Nancy didn't seem surprised that I knew this. "That didn't mean much to Penny."

"So Evan's divorce is because of Penny?"

"No, I don't think so," Nancy said. "Evan's always kept her at arm's length, as far as I can tell. But certainly, to Penny, the divorce was a good sign."

"So I'm being punished for leaving the party with him," I said. I looked out the door of my office. "First week here, and I'm already a target."

"Not just you."

"She sent Evan to Seattle for a week," I said. As it all sank in, my head pounded, and I craved a nap.

"You should probably end it, you know," Nancy said.

"End what?" I cried. "Nothing's happened."

Nancy tutted and left, closing the door after her.

I hunched over my punishment files for what seemed like eternity by the time Evan dropped in on his way out.

I stood up, but didn't go around my desk because I was afraid I would just fling myself at him. Stupid hang-over hormones.

"Um, no time for lunch?" I asked.

He shook his head.

"I'm sorry you have to go to Seattle," I said.

"I'll be back before you know it," he said.

"I'm really looking forward to Saturday."

"Oh, me, too. Believe me."

That was the moment when I should have given him a warm good-bye kiss to remember me by, but I felt the eyes of the whole office on me. So I shook his hand, once. "Have a good trip."

His middle finger caressed my palm, sending shivers up and down my entire body. "I won't," he said. "But coming back will be wonderful." Then he was gone.

ℰ✺ℰ✺

In a way, the sudden, difficult workload was a blessing. Some of the files were merely sloppy and required some straightening out, but others were convoluted and confusing, covered in tiny figures crossed out and re-written in a tidy, precise hand. Immersing myself in those files made it easier to keep myself from imagining licking dollops of cream off of Evan's freckled chest or from feeling paranoid about Penny. Time flew.

The upside to the day came after I got home. My cell rang as I was kicking off my heels. It was the livestock delivery company. "Your alpacas are on the truck and should arrive tomorrow."

"Oh, thank you," I cried. I allowed myself a little happy dance when I hung up.

Lew and Molly were excited that Seabiscuit and Secretariat were on their way, too. They had a little quarantine pasture set up for them and were now grilling me with questions about their lineage.

Molly stood outside the stall while Lew and I tended to Missy. After the interrogation, she nodded. "It sounds like you might have bought yourself a couple of winners there," she said. "At the very least, we don't have any of those bloodlines here on the farm. And we have a whole lot of Ambassador's daughters who need a date."

Lew chewed on his pipe a little. "As long as they have nice fiber and all four feet reach the ground, we might have some little studs on our hands."

"Really? I just bought them because they were cute."

"That's why everyone buys their first alpacas," Molly said. "You might just have really good taste in cute."

∽∾∾

Between unpacking my house and working on the convoluted files that Nancy kept bringing me from Ms. Alverez, the next day flew by. Evan even emailed me a cute little selfie of himself pointing to the Space Needle. I called Lew for updates at lunchtime, and then again in the afternoon, but my boys hadn't arrived.

Finally, as I was packing up for home, Lew called my cell. "Guess who's in the driveway?"

I sped home, even managing to go over twenty-five mph on the gravel roads. When I pulled up into the driveway, there were my boys, white Seabiscuit and brown Secretariat, munching on the lawn as Molly and Lew held their leads.

Alpacas are not dogs. In fact, they are more like cats than even horses. So, when I threw my arms around them, squealing in joy, their legs went stiff and they threw their heads up in alarm, even though they knew who I was. At least they were used to being handled, or they would have taken off down the driveway.

Molly shook her head. "You're going to scare them to death," she muttered.

"Oh, I know. I'm just so glad to see them," I said. I released their necks and looked in their huge, curious eyes. "Did you have a good trip, boys?"

Lew cleared his throat, so I looked up at him. "I— uh—have their paperwork here," he said.

"Yes?"

"These guys are pretty well bred," he began. "What did you say you paid for them?"

"About a grand for the pair," I said. "My Nana's friend Minnie set me up."

Lew and Molly exchanged a glance.

"Minnie Ambrose? Of Ambrose Alpacas?" Lew asked.

"Yes."

"That's a nice farm," he said looking at Secretariat closely.

"She gave you a hell of a deal," Molly said. "This is some good breeding in some nicely conformed animals. She must really like your Nana."

"Really?" I rubbed my boys' backs the way I knew

they liked. "I'll be sure to write her a thank-you note."

The quarantine pasture was a little ways off from the other pastures, on the other side of the barn. There was "no nose-to-nose contact," as Lew put it.

"Alpacas are like birds," he explained. "They are really stoic—when they are sick, you usually don't notice until they are nearly dead."

"…and have infected the whole herd," Molly added.

Seabiscuit and Secretariat didn't seem to mind being apart from the herd. They were knee-deep in fresh Oregon spring grass. They buried their heads in the tall forage and ignored us as we stood and watched them eat.

This was exactly what I needed to forget about work and Evan. The skies were still cloudy, but the air was warm enough that I could keep my jacket open as I leaned on a fence post and watched my guys nibble the new green shoots. They were already adapted to their new place in the world. I felt a gentle wave of envy for their peace of mind.

I called Nana after dinner.

"They're here," I said when she picked up.

"Oh, that's great, honey," she said. "Do they look okay? I've been so worried that I've cleaned the chicken coop twice to work off my nerves."

I laughed. "They're perfect. Right now they're eating green grass, wondering how they got so lucky."

"Wonderful." Nana's voice relaxed down a few notes, and I could almost hear her smile. "And how are you, darling?

"Oh, fine. You know how it is when you move."

"I haven't moved in fifty-five years," she reminded me. "And I'm only leaving this place feet first in a pine box."

"I don't blame you," I said. "Moving stinks. I can't find anything, I can't cook anything, and I feel like I'm living in a box factory."

"Well, tell me all about the parts of your new life that make it worth the move."

Leave it to Nana to make me focus on the positive. I told her about Lew and Molly, the beautiful farm, and about Missy's injury.

"…and Cody showed me how to use a diaper to bandage the wound," I said. "Can you imagine? Who knew you could use diapers as bandages?"

"Cody?" Nana asked.

Dammit. Nana had perfect pitch when it came to hearing something you didn't mean to say.

"Oh, Dr. Arden. He's the vet." I began picking the polish off of my left thumbnail. Maybe she would let it slip.

She didn't.

"Cody, huh?" she said. "He sounds…cute."

"I haven't said anything about how cute he is."

"You didn't have to," she said. "Have you gone out with him yet?"

I scoffed. "I'm sure he thinks I am a world-class dork. I fainted in the mud when I saw Missy's wound."

"But you recovered and wanted to help."

"I'm sure he's not interested," I said. "Besides, there's this guy at work—"

"Ooo! Two men?" Nana giggled in a way only old ladies and little girls can get away with. "Moving to the country has done you a world of good already."

"Nana." I probably said her name like an exasperated teenager. "I am not here to meet anyone. I thought you understood that."

"Oh, honey. I do understand," she said. "The thing is, once you start living life on your own terms, you start to attract people who like you because of the way you live."

"So, since I ran away to live alone on an alpaca ranch, I'll start meeting men who like girls who run away to live alone on alpaca ranches?"

"You'll meet all kinds," Nana said. "The ones who stay will like all sides of you, especially now that you're happy."

Later, as I picked at my "healthy" microwave pizza, Nana's words tumbled in my head, buffing and polishing the events of the week. She had given me a good excuse to date again—or, a flimsy justification, anyway. Perhaps it was raining men because I was a different person now that I wasn't mired in pain from the divorce or trying to escape Martin's memory. I had purged so much from my old life. Maybe I was a different, happier, more attractive person who could now attract men and not just predatory assholes.

I felt bad for trying to paint Evan into the "Panty-hose removing" category. He'd acted like a gentleman at every turn. True, he hadn't turned down any opportunities, and he was suave and forward, but he'd stopped when I asked him to. To be fair, I had agreed to go to his place, and I wasn't actually that drunk at the time.

Then my thoughts went to Dr. Cody Arden. Why was I thinking of him? Aside from being cute—Nana was right there—for some reason, I craved his approval. I felt warm, remembering the crinkle in his brown eyes when he smiled at me after I bandaged Missy's leg. I remembered his hand on my cheek when he was making sure I was okay after I fainted in the field. I remembered how I wanted to cry when I made a fool of myself in front of him.

Two men of interest in less than a week. I'd officially ended the man moratorium.

Chapter 5

Suddenly, it was Friday night and I was driving home, smiling to myself. Tomorrow, I was going to see Evan. I was so happy that I nearly missed the turn to my driveway.

He had sent me several chatty emails and pictures while he was gone. They were friendly and possibly suggestive. I'd re-read each one like a teen picking apart notes passed to her in class, trying to eke out every drop of meaning or innuendo before sending any replies. Then I fretted about the ways he could misinterpret what I'd written. Was "missing you," sincere, or was he being sardonic? Did "looking forward to Friday," mean that he was tired of traveling, or did he really want to see me? His last email confirmed the time for our date on Saturday.

As soon as I saw Lew in the driveway looking less

than cheerful, I knew something was wrong. "I think Angela's in labor," he said.

I frowned. "I thought no one was due for a couple weeks."

"You're right. She isn't due yet. Plus, she's a maiden—a first-time mom. We could be in for a long night."

"Damn."

I changed into my barn clothes, which I no longer bothered to wash after each trip outside. Then I went to the barn to see Angela. Lew and Molly stood by the pen, looking concerned. I peered in to see several pregnant alpacas.

"Um…"

"White one in the corner. She's chewing at her sides," Lew said. He stood quietly for a moment. "Ninety percent of the time alpacas give birth between sunrise and two p.m."

"So, night labor is…"

"Not normal."

"Angie's a new momma," Molly said. "Maidens don't always get the memo about morning births. A lot of them don't get the other memos, either."

"How to nurse a baby?"

"Or that the baby belongs to them."

"Hence the long night ahead," I said.

Angie threw her head up and looked alarmed. "There goes another contraction," Molly said. "Tch. She's so confused."

Angela was a big white alpaca who looked exactly as if she were built from marshmallows and toothpicks, except for her pointy ears, which now swung back and forth.

"Do we need to help her?" I asked.

Lew and Molly shook their heads.

"We need a rope and a chair," Lew said.

"Oh, God."

"First, you sit in the chair, and then we'll tie you to it with the rope!" He laughed at his own joke.

"Even in cases like Angie's," Molly explained, with a tolerant smile at Lew, "we rarely need to help with the actual birth. Plus, it can take a while. What we need to do is finish our chores and then make a pot of coffee."

It took me forty minutes to find my coffee maker after chores were done, so by the time I made it back to the barn with three mugs of Peet's special blend—a treat from Margot—Molly and Lew had shooed all the other alpacas to another stall so only Angie and one brown alpaca remained.

"That's Angie's mom, Laura," Lew explained. "Sometimes things go more smoothly if Mom's around."

We stood and watched as Laura lay down and chewed her cud while her daughter paced, stood, and cushed—or lay down—again and again. Finally, Molly looked at her watch.

"She's been at it for two hours."

"Best call the vet, then."

"Why?" I asked.

"If nothing's happened in two hours," Lew said as Molly stepped out of the barn with her cell, "could mean the baby is in the wrong position. We'll have to go in and see. First, we let the vet know what we're doing in case he needs to come out quick."

My stomach flipped. "Go in?"

Lew didn't notice. He was looking at the panting animal. "Have to reach in and see what's going on," he said. "The babies are supposed to come out feet first—preferably front feet. If Molly reaches in there and can't feel feet, we have a problem."

Molly returned with a jug of clear gel. She stepped into the stall and rolled up her shirtsleeves. Lew gently caught Angela and held her exactly as he'd held Missy when I changed her leg bandage. Molly poured a glob of gel onto her arm and hand and then reached up inside the alpaca's back end.

I held onto the rail and silently chanted, *Don't pass out. Don't pass out.*

"Shit," Molly said after a moment and pulled free. "All I felt was a lot of fur."

"Shit," Lew said. "Breach."

"Breach?"

"Butt first," Molly said. "Bad position. What's worse is that there isn't a lot of room in there."

"What do you mean?" I asked.

"My arm is too big," she said, holding up her meaty forearm. "I can't reach in far enough to catch a leg."

I looked at Lew who, though thin, had larger arms than Molly. Then I looked at my own arms. My mother once said I had elegant hands. "I'll try," I said.

"You?" Molly laughed like a seal barking. "I'm sorry, Meg, but you fainted at Missy's scrape!"

"Shut up," Lew snapped at Molly. "Lube her up. Come on, honey," he said to me. "We'll tell you what to feel for."

"First," Molly said. "Call the vet and tell him we need him." With her clean hand, Molly handed me the phone. My stomach flipped again.

When Dr. Arden answered, he sounded surprised to hear my voice. "Well, hello," he said.

"I need you," I said.

"Do you?"

"No, I mean, the alpaca has breeches, and I need to reach in and grab her foot."

"That does sound serious," he said. "I'll be right out. Take a deep breath," he added. "Do everything Lew and Molly tell you. I'll be there soon."

I hung up the phone and counted three deep breaths. "He's on his way," I said, walking into the stall.

"Okay," Lew said. "Roll up your sleeve."

With my arm bare up to my elbow, Molly poured the cold lubricating gel on and rubbed it around. Then she held Angie's tail out of the way. I stared at the swollen red alpaca vulva in front of me.

Don't lose it, don't lose it, don't lose it, I chanted in my brain.

"Now, just slide your hand in as far as it will go," Lew was saying. "You'll come to a hard lump with wet hair on it. That's the baby."

I put my clean hand on Angie's hip and, trying not to hyperventilate, slid my fingers and then my whole hand into the alpaca.

"Farther," Molly commanded.

I pushed my arm into the hot wetness. Then, next to the slick wetness, I felt fur. "I feel the baby," I cried.

"Good," said Lew. "Now, you're going to have to find the feet. Move your hand up and down until you find the tail. You know what a tail feels like, right?"

"Ow! Ow! It pinches!" Something, Angie, her insides were grabbing me, and one of my fingers was pinned between the baby and something very hard.

Molly held me and kept me from pulling out my arm. "It's just a contraction," she said, her voice quiet and close to my ear. "It'll be over in just a second, and it won't hurt you. Just wait for it." Her voice was calming, so I panted through the pressure on my arm until it passed. "Now, go find that tail quick. Angie's getting tired, and we need to get that baby out now!"

I pushed in deeper and felt up and down until I felt a skinny, furry snake. I seized it. "Found it," I said. "Do I pull?"

"No," Molly said. "Now, you need to find the leg. Run your hand down until you find a bend. A joint."

"Okay," I said. My face was now planted on Angie's soft, fluffy backend as I twisted my arm around inside her. "Found it."

"Look at her back leg," Lew said, pointing at Angie's leg. "Do you think you have a knee or a hock?"

"Hock."

"Good. Follow it down until you find the foot. You may have to reach a long way."

I wrapped my fingers around the leg and worked my

arm deeper and deeper, pushing my face harder against the alpaca's hip. I started to panic. This leg was impossibly long. "I can't find it!"

"It's there, it's there," Lew said. "Keep reaching."

Finally, there it was. Two toes, pointing down. "Got it."

"Attagirl," Lew said. Molly patted my back. "Now, pull it out."

I gave it a tug, but, of course, it was made of bone, not spaghetti. "How?"

"You'll have to push and pull up until the foot is kind of level with the opening, then draw it out slowly," Molly said. "Don't force anything yet."

I did was I was told, and, weirdly, I could feel the baby shifting inside as I pushed and pulled. Then I pulled out a tiny black foot attached to a furry white leg. "Oh, God," I said, leaning against Molly. "I did it."

Molly smiled. "Yes, you did. Good job, Meg. Now, we need to get the other one out."

The second leg proved far more difficult than the first to extract. The little creature inside did not want to cooperate and kept pulling its leg out of my hand. Angela was in pain and frightened, and I swear she kept trying to break my arm with her contractions. Blood dripped from where my arm plunged into the animal. I was hot, but I couldn't take off my sweatshirt. It was dark, too, despite the dusty bare bulb swinging overhead.

At Angela's next contraction, I lost hold of the little foot again. "Damn," I cried and pulled my arm out. I rested my clean arm and head against Angela's hip and began sobbing. "I can't do it. Are they going to die?"

"I don't think so," Molly said and handed me a towel. "Clean up and sit over there. Cody should be here any minute, and he'll have the baby out in no time."

"He's a pro," Lew agreed. He let Angela go. She immediately cushed and dropped her head to the ground, groaning a little. "Poor thing's exhausted," he muttered, moving slowly out of the stall.

I sat on a cold bale of hay, my sticky arm sore and wrapped in a scratchy towel. Molly handed me one of the now lukewarm mugs of coffee. I drank it, anyway. We all listened for the crunch of pickup tires on gravel.

We didn't have to wait long before we heard the vet's vehicle flying up the driveway. He skidded to a stop outside the door, shining the headlights into the stalls, blinding us. Dr. Arden emerged from the glare like a saving angel, already unbuttoning his shirt.

Lew managed a grin. "It's cold in here, Cody. Leave your shirt on."

The vet smiled. "Not *that* cold. Besides, my mom got me this shirt." He tossed the button-down onto the bale beside me. "Hi," he said.

"Hi." His bare shoulders almost made me forget where we were.

He didn't forget. He turned and took a look at Angela. "Did Meg get the back foot out?" he asked.

Lew nodded. "Yeah. She worked that leg out like a pro."

"Good job!" Dr. Arden smiled at me. "Right, then. See if you can get her up again."

I went in with Molly and Lew and stood at Angela's hip, grasping fistfuls of fleece to keep her from lying down again. I had a perfect view of Cody working, but that meant he had a perfect view of my filthy torso covered in God knows what.

His hands and arms did not seem particularly small, but he was able to get into the tight spot I'd been working in and find the foot. "Come on," he muttered as he worked the leg. He nodded slowly as if he were thinking, and I could imagine him maneuvering the leg as I had. I found myself nodding, too.

"Come on," I whispered.

Finally, he looked up at me and flashed a gleeful smile. "Got it," he cried and pulled out the other tiny foot. We all cheered. "Now, let's get her out."

The vet stood, grasped the little feet, and gently leaned back. The long white legs came out easily enough, but he had to wait for a contraction to pull out the little hips and another for the shoulders. When the head and front feet came out, I was thoroughly in love.

The baby was creamy white and covered in curls. Dr. Arden pried its mouth open, checked the umbilical cord, and peeked under the tail.

"It's a girl," he said. His voice sounded funny, but I didn't think about it.

When he set her down, she raised her head on her long wobbly neck and looked around, blinking.

I dropped to my knees next to her and cooed, "Oh my God. She's beautiful."

The cria looked at me and swung her little ears toward me. I reached out to touch her new wetness when Dr. Arden caught my arm and pulled me back.

"Wait, Meg," he said. "Come over here a moment."

I stood. "Of course. They need time to bond." Then I looked at the other three people with a slow realization that something was wrong. Not one of them looked happy. Dr. Arden pulled me into a corner and the four of us stood and looked at the cria as Angela sniffed it curiously. "Is—is something wrong, Dr. Arden?"

"Call me Cody," he said. His hand was still on my arm.

"Cody?" I looked into his cool brown eyes and his knitted brows.

"Meg, this cria isn't going to live."

"What?" I looked from Cody to the tiny creature in the stall. It looked alive to me. "Why not?"

"It has some birth defects," he said quietly.

"Birth defects?" I looked at Molly and Lew. Their faces told the same story. Lew's was drawn and grim, and Molly was silently crying, tears streaming down her cheeks.

"It has Choanal atresia. The nasal passages are closed off. It won't be able to breathe while it nurses."

"How? How do you know?"

"It's breathing through its mouth," Cody pointed out. "See?"

I looked at the little baby panting through its open mouth. "I thought it was tired from the birth."

"Is surgery an option?" Lew asked quietly.

"I'll pay for surgery," I exclaimed. "Let's do surgery."

"I'd have to do a thorough examination to see if surgery is even an option," Cody said, looking into my eyes. "But I doubt it would do any good." I held my breath and wished, recognizing that look on a veterinarian's face, but it didn't change what he said next. "There is no anus, either, Meg. It can't eat or defecate. It's going to die."

I stared at the baby in the stall. It was trying to stand. "But she's alive now," I whimpered. "Where there's life, there's hope, right?"

When he looked in my eyes and shook his head, I couldn't feel my legs anymore. I collapsed into his arms, sobbing for the second time that night, and felt him ease me onto a bale of hay. He cradled me against his skin and held me while I cried. When he was stroking my hair, I thought of Nana when I showed up on her doorstep. I cried harder.

"Can you walk?" Cody whispered in my ear.

I shook my head and sobbed some more. I felt him lift me up in his still-shirtless arms and carry me across the barnyard to my house. Molly came along to open the door and pull off my shoes when we got inside. Cody set me on my feet and pressed me to him again. I felt better resting my cheek against his warm chest and smelling his scent of animal and man.

He pulled away. "I'll do my best," he said. Then he was gone.

I stood dumbly blinking at the door Cody had left through, so Molly took me back to my bedroom, helped me out of my filthy barn clothes, and pushed me into a hot shower. When I got out, I found a pair of pajamas laid out on a box near my bed. The message was clear: We'll take care of this. You go to bed.

Instead, I put on the pajamas and stood at the window that had the best view of the barn. I saw the lights were still on and the shadows on the wall meant that people were still in there. I crossed my fingers and toes like a third-grader and prayed, which was something I didn't do much. But I prayed and prayed for the gleaming white baby in the barn, offering whole Sundays devoted to church, swearing off men—again—or coffee, or a year's salary or anything at all, just so that the little baby in the stall would survive.

Finally, the lights in the barn were switched off. I saw the three people gather in the headlights of the truck. I glanced at the clock. It was 2:30 in the morning.

Two people headed toward the trailer: Lew and Molly. The other headed toward the house where I stood next to the window. I saw that he had put on his shirt and jacket and scrubbed his face and hands with the cold barn water so he glowed. I met him at the door, barefoot, wet-haired, and in puppy pajamas. I smiled and crossed my fingers.

He took one look at me and closed his eyes. "Shit," he said.

"What?"

"Can I come in?"

I stepped out of the doorway. Cody kicked off his boots and left them outside. He refused coffee, so I led him to the couch and we sat. Then he looked up at me with those beautiful brown eyes again.

"We had to put her down, Meg."

"But—but you were in there so long," I said. "I thought for sure—"

"I was looking for any possible way out other than this," he said. "But there were simply too many things wrong."

"Like what?" I asked.

He looked up at my sharp tone. "Well, besides the CA and anal deformity, there was a pronounced heart murmur and the breathing was really wet sounding." He reached out to take my hand. "The cria was going to die in a matter of hours, maybe live one day before it began to suffer and then die in pain," he said.

"She could have lived a whole day?" I said, snatching my hand away. "And you *killed* her?"

"Meg," he said, reaching for my hand again. "It was going to die in horrible pain. The only thing we could ethically do was end its pain sooner rather than later."

"Nobody asked me," I spat, jerking my arm away again.

"No, that was a mistake," Cody admitted, putting his hands in his lap. "We thought you were asleep. Lew, Molly, and I had a long discussion about exploratory surgeries and other options, but really, Meg, any of those had a slim-to-nil chance of fixing anything. They had a much better chance of putting a miserable little creature through more unnecessary misery. That's why we—"

"Killed her." I had never been so angry at one person

before. Martin had destroyed me, but I was a full-grown woman who could fight back. That little creature was just trying to breathe, and had no fight. I felt repulsed that I had taken comfort in this monster's arms. "You. Get out of my house. Now."

"Meg, I—"

"Out! Now!" I stood and pointed at the door.

Cody stood slowly. "I understand why you're mad at me," he said. "When you calm down, remember this: It just kills me when I have to put an animal down. But it makes me feel worse when I have to watch it suffer just to satisfy an owner's inability to see past her own selfish needs."

I stood frozen as Cody wiped his face. Was he crying? He looked up at me one last time with red eyes, said, "I'm sorry," and left.

I lowered my arm and listed to the sound of his footsteps on the gravel and the growl of the pickup's engine as he drove slowly down my long driveway. Then the darkness of the country closed in, and I felt as if I was in the only sad puddle of light in the world. When I crawled into bed, I realized I had left a window open and the cold night air was seeping in. I sat up to close it when I noticed a tiny sound.

Listening, I realized it was spring peepers: tiny frogs. I lay back on my pillows, pulled up another blanket, and listened to the little creature's mating cries until I fell asleep.

ᥱᥱᥱ

I didn't get out of bed until noon. I didn't care about missing morning chores, I didn't care about the sun streaming onto my face, promising a beautiful day. I was wallowing in misery and I was not ready to face the world.

Of course I'd lost pets before. I'd held a dog as the needle put him to sleep, and I'd searched the alleyways for my lost cat only to find her dead in someone's back yard. I hadn't blamed the vet who had put my friend out of his misery or the car that had hit my kitty. Their deaths hadn't sent me into a spiral of depression like this. But then, they hadn't been babies, and I hadn't felt betrayed.

I was grieving for the brief life in the barn, but I knew Cody wasn't to blame. He was 100% right—it would have been far worse to make an animal suffer just because I wasn't strong enough to accept its death. I had behaved awfully. I was totally ashamed. I burrowed deeper into the covers that now felt scratchy and punitive.

I had to apologize to him.

Instead, I dragged my butt out of bed, grabbed a package of cookies, and nuked a cup of day-old coffee in the microwave. Then I took a lawn chair and dragged it into the alpaca pasture. I plunked into the chair and ate cookie after cookie, washing them down with the bitter coffee. I had forgotten to add sugar.

The sun felt good, warming my skin and making my hair hot. The grass smelled good, and I was surrounded by little things leafing out. Daffodils were erupting along the fence line, but the trees were only just starting to flower. I realized that the seasons were at least a month behind Berkeley where the cherry trees had been in full bloom when I'd moved.

I allowed myself to sink into the wonder of early spring, and I felt better. A smile crept onto my face, testing the waters. A bird let loose a liquid warble. I took a deep breath and closed my eyes.

When I opened them, tears.

Angela had entered the pasture, followed by the rest of the herd. Her mother, Laura, stuck close to her daughter as the herd passed them and began grazing.

Angela, trailed by her mom, sniffed along the fence, investigating every corner, peering under the bushes and circling tree trunks. She was humming a question over and over: Are you here? Where? Where? Are you here?

I wanted to take her in my arms and tell her how sorry I was, how I missed the little angel, too. I cried because not only had I failed to save the baby, but I couldn't even comfort her mom.

When I looked up, I saw a shadow standing over me. I turned to find Lew watching Angela, too. He smiled down at me and put a hand on my shoulder.

"She'll probably look for a couple days before she gives up." He squeezed my shoulder. "In a week she'll forget the whole thing."

"Really?"

"It's the one thing I envy them for," he said. "They live entirely in the present. That's why it's cruel to put them through too many painful procedures. Unless it extends their life pain-free for a long time, it's basically torture." He sighed. "But they also recover from trauma so well because they aren't living in the past, re-living the experience over and over. You know?" He looked at me and smiled again. "Aren't there experiences you wish you could forget so you could just get on with your life?"

"Me? Nah."

I waved my hand as if nothing bothered me. He wasn't buying it. So I offered him a cookie from my half-eaten sack.

"Don't mind if I do." Lew sat in the grass beside my chair, and we munched and watched Angela and Laura. Eventually, the older alpaca began grazing while the other continued to search.

"Did you hear from Cody this morning?" I asked.

Lew was quiet a moment. "Yes," he said. "He called first thing to follow up." He looked at me. "He said you were furious last night."

"I threw him out of the house," I admitted, looking at my feet. "It wasn't really about him—it wasn't all about the cria. He didn't deserve me throwing him out like that, especially when he did the right thing." I took a deep breath. "I owe him an apology."

Lew nodded. "Cody's been doing this a long time. He knows that losing an animal unleashes all sorts of emotions in people. Still," he said. "I'm sure he'd appreciate an apology."

A group of alpacas walked up to us and, after sniffing us to their satisfaction, they began grazing at our feet.

"I'll call him," I said. "Tonight."

Of course, I didn't call Cody that night. As soon as I found my cell phone still in my car where I'd left it amid the confusion of the night before, I remembered my date with Evan. He'd left three messages since he had landed around ten p.m. the night before just to confirm the time of our date and say how excited he was. He left the most recent message while I had been sitting in the pasture, and he sounded a little worried. I began to call him back, fully intending to cancel because I felt like shit, and I was sure I looked it, too.

A text message popped up as I stood formulating an excuse that didn't involve either a dead baby or me lying awake all night in a shame-spiral over my two-year-old divorce. The message read: *3 hrs till our date! Can't w8! Ironing shirt.*

I laughed. It felt good. Maybe instead of moping around my house not unpacking, I could go out with someone who wanted to make me happy. Someone who could make me laugh. Suddenly, I wanted to give it a try, so I typed, *C U there!* and wandered into my bedroom. I hadn't unpacked all my clothes yet, and those I had un-packed were wrinkled beyond recognition. I had no idea where my iron was.

I dug around until I found a dress with a large-scale flower print that actually looked as if it were designed to be wrinkled. Then I begged off of chores with Lew who winked at me lasciviously when I admitted I had a date. I wasn't going to take another shower, so I pulled on my lucky headband with the pretty ribbon and then applied some make-up. After scrutinizing myself in the mirror, I hoped that the restaurant was on the dark side.

As I drove into town, I resolved not to mention dead

babies, shirtless veterinarians, or divorce-inspired shame spirals. That was a pretty long list of "don'ts" for me, but I could do it. Right? I could fake interest and laugh on cue with the best of them. I also resolved to go home—my home—after the meal. I knew I was still too emotional to trust myself back at Evan's place.

Then I saw Evan waiting for me in a quiet booth in the back of a dimly lit, romantic bistro. I knew I was in trouble when he looked up, smiled, and walked over to meet me. By the time he got to my side, my smile was no longer faked.

He raised my hand to his lips. "You look wonderful."

I believed him.

Through dinner, I laughed and chatted and almost convinced myself that nothing out of the ordinary had occurred in his absence. I tried to keep from flirting too outrageously, and I willed myself to at least be coy about going home with him. Evan hung on my every word and watched me with those blue eyes. He also kept refilling our wine glasses. I didn't stop him. Feeling appreciated and drunk was better by far than the way I felt last night.

Finally, we stood in the cool night air outside the restaurant, laughing at something that wasn't really that funny. I closed my eyes, took a deep breath, and found the scent of some early flower faintly perfuming the air. I exhaled, feeling my warm breath on my lips. I opened my eyes and found Evan watching me.

"Do that again," he whispered.

I smiled and closed my eyes. I hadn't finished exhaling when I felt Evan's soft kiss on my mouth and his arms wrapping around me. "Let's take a walk."

He dropped an arm around my shoulders, and we crossed the street to a city park where a fountain bubbled to itself. We drunkenly negotiated the stairs made slick with overspray and then walked toward the river. He steered us to a great spreading oak near the water's edge and leaned me against it. Then he looked down and kissed me. Each time he touched me, my heart raced, and I found myself reaching for his face or slipping my cold hands under his coat and sliding my fingers against the warmth of the shirt pressed against his skin.

I was still cold and shivered. He wrapped me in his coat, and I laid my head against his chest. "Come home with me," he whispered into my hair.

Rational thought was drowned out by Evan's heart pounding in one ear and my heart pounding in the other. Together, they drowned out the sadness and shame from last night.

"Okay," I said.

We left our cars and walked to Evan's apartment. Had I been more sober and not as lustful, I might have found this proximity suspicious. Instead, it seemed infinitely convenient.

It took a while for us to get there since we stopped every half block or so to kiss, but eventually we made it to the door. We dropped our coats on the floor and flopped on the couch.

I was fumbling with Evan's shirt buttons when he cupped my chin in his hand and smiled at me. "You know," he said. "I have more wine and some candles—"

"That's sweet," I said, and kissed him. Then I went back to work on his buttons.

Evan caught my wrists in his hands and looked me in the eye, a little crease crinkling between his eyes. "I'm a fool for saying this," he said. "But you seem a little…off tonight."

"Am I coming on too strong?"

"A little," he admitted. "But that's not it. Is something bothering you?"

Was something bothering me? "I don't want to talk about it," I said finally. "It's not on the list of approved first-date topics."

Evan nodded. "Well," he said. "Either you can look at this as our second date, or you can accept that going home with me isn't really first-date behavior, either. At least, not where I come from." He tucked some hair behind my ear. "What's eating you?" he asked gently.

"It's not second date material, either." But I was drunk. I was exhausted. I was sad and weary. I wanted to talk. "I lost a baby alpaca yesterday—last night."

"Lost?"

"It was born with birth defects and had to be put down." I had been praying that I could say that sentence without breaking down, but I dissolved into tears, anyway. For the second time in twenty-four hours, a man gathered me into his arms and let me weep my grief into his bare chest.

After I'd cried myself out, Evan wiped the tears from my cheeks. "The bathroom is at the top of the stairs if you want to clean up."

"Okay," I said. I went upstairs and pressed a cold washcloth to my eyes both to reduce the puffiness and wash off the remaining mascara. No point in maintaining that illusion, I thought. I ran my fingers through my short blonde curls and assessed my image. I looked exactly like someone who'd just finished a crying jag. "Just go home," I ordered my reflection, which nodded humbly.

Evan was waiting on the couch, but stood when I stepped into the room. "Are you all right?"

"Yeah." I picked up my shoes and my coat from the floor. "I should go."

He was next to me in two steps and took my hand in both of his. "Why?"

"Oh, I think the mood is gone," I said.

"Not for me," he said, kissing my knuckles. "Is it gone for you?"

"Not really," I said, feeling little zings where his lips had been. "But I'm a mess, and an emotional wreck, and…" I trailed off.

"Listen," Evan said. "You are a beautiful mess. Stay. Please?"

I was suddenly very, very tired. The prospect of driving home in the dark to my cold, empty house paled in comparison to spending an evening with this warm, funny, concerned man who might at least keep me from diving back into that dark, depressing pit I was in last night. So I nodded and let him lead me back to the couch where he collected me into his lap like a child. I rested my head against his chest and listened to his heart again as he smoothed my hair.

"Do you want to talk about it?" he asked.

I shook my head.

"Can I ask a question?"

I nodded.

"What's an alpaca?"

Chapter 6

O ver the course of the next hour, Evan lit candles and opened the wine while I told him the story of the little alpaca. I did have to begin with an explanation of what an alpaca actually is before I launched into the story. I decided to omit the part about fishing out the little feet. Instead I told him I "assisted in the birth." I also left out the part about crying into Cody's shoulder and then throwing him out of the house.

When I was done, Evan took my hand. "You've been busy since you got here, haven't you?"

"I suppose I have." I watched him caress my fingers. "You really didn't know what an alpaca was?"

"No idea," he said. "Grew up in Portland in the 'burbs. Never had a pet as a kid. Sort of never paid attention to animals, I guess." He massaged my hand and fingers one by one.

"I was horse-crazy as a girl, but I haven't had any pets since college. My ex didn't like them."

"Let's not bring up the exes," Evan said, laying a finger on my lips. He tipped my chin up and kissed me. "Bad luck."

He leaned in again and I melted into the kiss, the last of my resolve dissolving. Why had I been so intent on going home? Hadn't I wanted Evan since the instant I saw him?

He buried his face in my neck. "I really want to take you upstairs."

After a beat, I said, "Okay."

He looked into my eyes. "Really?"

I nodded and smiled. "I need this—you."

"Forgive me if I don't ask again." Evan stood and led me by the hand up to his room.

Despite the assertive way Evan had been pursuing me, his touch was soft, almost tentative. He pulled down my dress and caressed my skin, kissing my neck and shoulders. He slid my bra off and worshiped my breasts. By the time we were naked in bed, I had lost track of everything but my skin and his.

I was relieved. I wasn't in the mood for passionate pawing of any kind. I needed comfort. I needed to be pampered, taken care of. Evan knew this.

More than once after my divorce, I'd awakened next to a relative stranger, feeling a little cheap. I'd tried to reassure myself with the pizza/sex analogy: even bad pizza is still pizza. I stopped dating when I realized I was tired of so much bad pizza.

As we cuddled in his cool sheets, I decided that if I'd met Evan in Berkeley, I would still be there. When I woke in the morning, I found Evan still curled around me protectively. I glanced at the clock and swore. I pulled myself away and, pulling on a shirt—his—I padded down the stairs to find my cell phone.

"Lew? I'm sorry. I'm going to miss morning chores."

"Indeed?" Lew said. I could hear his smile crackle over the line. "Everything okay?"

"Things are fine, *Dad*." I laughed. "I'll be home later."

"You sound better," Lew said. "We were worried yesterday."

"Thanks," I said. "See you later."

"Who was that?"

I turned to find Evan standing on the landing in a robe. He cocked an eyebrow at me.

"I just had to call the farm hands," I explained. "To let them know I'd miss morning chores."

He smiled. "Oh, good. I was afraid you were calling your other boyfriend to set up a date for tonight."

I laughed. "I've only been here a couple weeks. When would I have had time to find other men to date?"

"Right answer," he said.

Then he took me into his arms and kissed me hard, and we had sex on the living room floor. That time, it was the sweaty, pawing kind, which was just fine with me.

We shared a shower and then went out to brunch. I had to wear the same wrinkled dress from last night, but I tried to convince myself that I looked like the rest of the post-church brunch eaters and not like the "walk of shame" poster child.

Over eggs Benedict, I picked up a thread of last night's conversation that had been bothering me. "So, you have no interest in animals at all?"

"Not really," Evan said. "Airplanes, trucks, yes. I play lots of Risk online with my friends. Cute, fuzzy critters? Not so much. Maybe it's a boy thing." He searched my face. "That's not a problem, is it?"

"Oh, no," I said brightly. "No problem at all. I mean, we just started—this."

He sat back from his omelet and crossed his arms. "Why did you move from the city to a llama ranch?"

"Alpaca," I corrected automatically. "I needed to get away from my old life. Those memories."

He nodded, so I left it at that.

"Why an alpaca ranch?"

I sighed and told him of visiting Minnie's ranch and Seabiscuit and Secretariat and the realization that I needed something other than another man in my life—I needed my own life.

"Do you understand?"

He smiled. "If Minnie had been raising ostriches, do you think you'd be neck-deep in feathers right now?"

I shook my head. "I don't think so. I did my research. My long-term goal is to make the ranch into a business."

"Then why work at B and W?"

I shrugged. "I knew I wasn't going to make a go of

the ranch right away. Besides, I like to keep up in my field."

Evan reached across the table and took my hand. "I'm glad you decided to work for us," he said.

"Me, too."

✑✎✑✎

When I stepped into my house later that day, I regarded the piles of boxes and disordered furniture that had seemed so overwhelming yesterday. I changed out of my dress into jeans and a tee shirt, tied my curls back with a kerchief, and set to work.

I unpacked the rest of my clothes, located my iron, and got the worst of the wrinkles out of the outfits I was likely to wear soonest.

Then I tackled the kitchen, making decisions about pot location and appliance territories. By the time I was hungry enough for dinner, I was ready to move the living room furniture around so that the sun didn't glare on the television.

The setting sun reminded me it was time for chores, so I pulled on my barn shoes and walked outside. When I stepped into the barn, I blushed under Lew and Molly's gazes. Lew, of course, had a lecherous, amused grin on his face and, though Molly's look wasn't exactly reproachful, it was more severe than Lew's.

"Did you have fun?" Lew asked.

"Yes, yes, I did," I said. "Please, no further questions."

Molly nodded, and suddenly I knew that she and Lew had spent the whole day speculating who I had been with and what I had been doing. I must be the most interesting thing to happen here since Sandy's divorce, I thought. "So, is this Evan boy nice?" she asked.

I looked at her with my mouth agape. "Who? How did you know?"

Lew poked Molly in the ribs, and she actually giggled. "Rosie called this morning after church," he explained. "She saw you at brunch looking inordinately happy."

I felt myself blush again. "So the whole town knows?"

Lew shrugged. "There's only one place to get a nice breakfast on a Sunday morning around here," he said. "You're not the first to show up there in a Saturday night dress."

I felt a deep pang of nostalgia for the anonymity of a big city. "Holy shit," I said. "I am in so much trouble tomorrow."

"Workplace romances don't usually work out," Molly said.

I sat on a hay bale and put my head in my hands. "It's not just that. My boss has a thing for Evan."

"Really?" Molly said. She exchanged a glance with Lew. "I hadn't heard that part of it."

"I'm such an idiot," I said with a half-laugh. "I'm so weak. I kept telling myself to go home last night. I even tried to cancel the date because I knew it wasn't a good idea!"

"But you had fun?" Molly asked.

"Yes," I said. "It was one of the best dates of my life."

"And you want to see him again?"

"Yes. More than I've wanted to see a man in a long, long time."

"Well, then," said Lew. "I suppose that's worth a little trouble at work, then."

"But what if I get fired?" I said, suddenly voicing my unspoken fears. "How will I pay the mortgage? Or your salaries?"

Lew laughed a little. It was a reassuring sound. "This place was profitable before you came, Meg. If you lose your job—which hasn't happened yet—we'll manage."

I smiled. "How did you get so wise?"

Molly snorted. "Lew isn't wise," she said. "He's full of shit. But we love that about him, don't we?"

∽∾∽∾

On Monday I made it into my office without making eye contact with anyone, partly by arriving ridiculously early and shutting my door. The office had a surreal quality to it, partly because of the hour and vacancy, but also because the last time I had seen it was before my baby alpaca had died, before I had wept into the bare chests of two different men and become the talk of the town. It had been quite a weekend.

By the time Nancy, Penny, and the others filed in at nine, I'd been there an hour and had finished off three files I hadn't been able to focus on Friday afternoon. I did my best turtle impression, bent over my desk and looking so busy that several people who stopped by took one look in my little office window, thought the better of interrupting me, and left.

Even Evan's knock was tentative, but I smiled and waved him in. I stood up and he closed the door behind him, then he caught me around the waist and stole a kiss. I pulled back and rubbed the lipstick off his mouth with my thumb.

"Don't do that," I whispered with a smile and retreated behind my desk.

"Why not?"

I frowned at him. "You don't want people talking, do you?"

Evan sat in my guest chair and tilted his head like a confused dog. "You think people are talking about us?"

"I know they are."

He looked over his shoulder at my closed door. "Who?"

"My farmhands, for starters," I whispered again. Then I realized what I was doing and I forced myself to speak normally. "Their daughter saw us at brunch on Sunday."

"Has anyone here said anything?"

"I don't know," I said. "I'm avoiding everyone at this point."

"Aha," Evan said, nodding slowly. "I get it. You don't want anyone to know."

"Well, it's not that—"

"No, no, I can tell you're embarrassed by me. I'll just go."

I laughed. "Sit down, silly. That's not it. It's just that, you know, workplace romances aren't usually a good idea."

"You remember Ross and Danielle? They met here when he started. Married."

"Oh?"

"And Ace and Julia."

"So, dating among employees is *de rigueur* here?"

"If you mean that it's common, then, yes."

"So, have you dated anyone else here?" I asked, watching how he'd answer.

He shrugged. "That's for me to know," he said, winking.

"If you're going to tease me, get out." I tried to pout, but ended up laughing.

Evan leaned across my desk and kissed my forehead. "See you for lunch?"

"Absolutely."

He tapped on my door again at noon. I stood in my doorway, feeling paranoid, having spent the morning wondering not only which couples at B and W had hooked up at the office, but also how many of them were now whispering about me and Evan. When I stepped out of the doorway, I was sure I felt several pairs of eyes on me, and I thought I saw people looking away as my gaze swept the cubicles, so when Evan reached for my hand, I pulled away.

"Outside," I whispered.

He shrugged and led the way though the cubicles to the front doors. He seemed so nonchalant, which made me relax a little. Perhaps I was overreacting in a prudish, school-girl way. After all, we were adults, and we weren't hurting anyone. I allowed myself to admire Evan's cute ass as we neared the front door. I smiled as we passed Nancy's desk, but she caught my eye and gave me a single headshake. I started and tripped on the rubber welcome mat inside the door, so I fell into Evan's arms just outside. He gathered me up like that had been his plan all along and kissed me as the big glass door swung shut on Nancy's visage.

"So much for keeping this under the radar," I said.

"I'm not a spy plane," Evan said, draping an arm across my shoulders. "I'm a man with a beautiful girl who wants a burrito. How's that sound?"

"How did you know I wanted a burrito?" I laughed. "Taco truck or sit-down?"

"Oh, taco truck all the way."

I was laughing as we walked past Nancy's desk again at one o'clock. I slapped his hand away playfully when he grabbed for mine in the foyer. "Not in the office," I said. "Let's try to be professionals, shall we?"

Evan stepped into my office for a carne asada-flavored kiss. He brushed a curl from my forehead and smiled when it bounced back. "Let's go out to dinner tonight."

I stepped back. "Not tonight. I have to unpack in the worst way. Let's do Thursday instead."

Evan groaned. "Thursday is so far away."

"Show some restraint," I said. "We'll have lunch tomorrow." I kissed him and patted his butt as he walked out the door.

I left my door open for the rest of the afternoon, smiling at the people who stopped to ask a question or say hello. I was in a buoyant mood when Nancy arrived, but that evaporated once I saw what was in her hands.

"Oh, no! Are those all for me?"

"I'm afraid so," she said. She set the files on my desk and then nodded towards Penny's office.

"If she's mad at me, why doesn't she just say so?" I said, poking the files with the eraser of my pencil. "I don't like being punished without a trial."

Nancy shrugged. "The way you two were carrying on today, I'm not surprised."

I felt myself blush. "I've been trying to keep it discrete, but Evan says that office dating is pretty well accepted here."

"I suppose it's all right for the ones in the cubes," Nancy sniffed. "I think the standard is a little higher for those of you with doors."

"I should have expected that," I said. Then I sighed and opened the file on top. "I'll just bear my cross and kept quiet about it."

"That might not be enough," Nancy said. "If you don't want this to get worse, you should probably stop seeing him."

I bit my lip. "You're probably right, Nancy. But I'm not ready to do that."

"Suit yourself," she said. "Don't say I didn't warn

you." She swept from the room somehow taking my buoyancy with her.

"Shit." I stood and shut my door, leaning against it for a moment. All of a sudden, I wanted to see Evan for dinner and more, but the little voice in my head said, *No!* very firmly. I sighed again and sat behind my desk, steeling myself for the task of sorting and trying to remedy the convoluted data in the pile of cases on my desk. Damn Penny and her backhanded punishment.

After that day, I needed to relax. When I got home, I fixed myself a stiff G and T. Then I went to the pasture, dragging my lawn chair, while carrying my drink in one hand and my book under my armpit. *I am getting good at this*, I thought as I settled in to enjoy the creatures and the spring evening.

I was about two chapters into my book when an unfamiliar blue pickup truck rumbled up my driveway. It passed my house and parked in front of Lew and Molly's trailer. The door swung open and out hopped Rosie, Lew's daughter. She waved to me and strode down the hill.

"Hi!" she said when she was close. "You look more comfortable now than you did in the supermarket."

"Thanks," I said, rising from my chair.

"Which one's the patient?"

I scanned the pasture and pointed to Missy's black butt. "Over there."

"Thought so. Blue vet wrap gives it away." She nodded as she watched the alpaca step forward to some fresh grass. "No limp. You guys did a good job."

"Thanks, again." I looked up at her truck: blue with duallies. I was getting the hang of this country thing. "Visiting Lew?" I asked.

"Yup." Rosie looked at their trailer. "Gotta love the old coot, doncha?"

"I'd sure be lost without him," I admitted.

We watched the alpacas for a moment while I wished and prayed that Rosie wouldn't bring up Sunday morning. I knew what she was thinking, though, by the same lopsided grin that Lew gave me.

"So…brunch with Evan Ridgefield, huh?" she said.

"Yeah." I tried not to look embarrassed, but I had a feeling that Rosie could see straight through me.

"That is a nice piece of beef," she said. "If I were dating, MMMmmm-mm!"

"Married?"

"Widowed," she said. She held out her hand as Secretariat walked up for a sniff. "Fell off a green-broke stallion into a ditch."

"Oh, I'm sorry."

"It was a long time ago." Rosie shrugged. "I haven't had time to do the dating thing, and I don't really see the point right now, either."

I nodded. "I had almost a year-long man moratorium after my divorce."

Rosie rubbed Seabiscuit who came up for some love, too. "You know who'd I have if I could? Cody Arden."

"The vet?" At once I was transported back to the cold barn where I had been comforted by his warm skin.

"Sure," Rosie said. "Actually, we did date a little before I met my husband, but it didn't work out. We're both a little too dedicated to our work, you know? Anyway, I know that the two of us wouldn't work, but that doesn't keep me from thinking about that curly black hair at night." She grinned wickedly again. "Don't you think he's cute?"

Again, Cody's strong arms encircled me and his bare chest pressed against my wet cheek as he eased my grief over the lost little one. I remembered how he smelled like the best parts of a barn—the hay, the feed, the alpacas—and of clean, sweet soap. I felt my color rise. Then I remembered the ending of the night when I threw him out of my house, and I felt my color drain again. I still hadn't apologized—

"Meg?"

"He's got his good points," I managed to say. I hoped that Rosie couldn't read minds, but I felt certain she could. "So does Evan," I finished, trying to be diplomatic—or something.

"This is true," she said. She paused and bumped my hip with her own. "That was a pretty dress you were wearing to brunch."

I laughed. "It was prettier before it spent the night on his bedroom floor."

"So much for not dating, huh?"

"Hell, it had been almost a year." The two of us laughed the way I laughed with Beth and Margot. "Wanna come in for some coffee?"

"Sure," Rosie said. "Dad won't mind. He knows where I am."

⌒⌒⌒

Rosie was frowning at me over her steamy mug. "What do you mean you're afraid of horses?" she asked. "You just said you used to trade stall cleaning for lessons."

"When I was a teenager," I said. "I—I was injured by a horse, so I quit riding when I was seventeen."

"Oh. What happened?"

I stirred my coffee and pondered where to start the story. "The short version is that a very angry horse decided to kill the rake I was holding. He broke my leg, and it took a whole summer to heal. I still have occasional nightmares of black hooves coming for me."

Rosie clucked sympathetically. "No one could convince you to get back on after you were well?"

I shook my head. "I went to college and then moved to a city, so no one ever asked. Not that I sought it out."

"Well," said Rosie, leaning across my kitchen table. "Consider this me asking you to come out and ride again. That'll get those dreams under control."

I smiled. "That's kind of you—"

"No, no," she cut me off. "I'm not going to take no for an answer. I'm even going to get my Dad to nag you until you make the trip out."

I rolled my eyes. I imagined Lew bringing up riding every three seconds until eternity. He would do it, too. "Fine," I relented. "Don't sic Lew on me."

⌒⌒⌒

The next evening as I arrived home, I was surprised again by a visitor. This time, the vet's truck followed me up the driveway.

Holy crap. How do I look?

I glanced at myself in the rearview mirror, heart pounding. I looked tired from hunching over the frustrating pile of files on my desk, but at least I was in my work clothes and had some lipstick left. I looked good enough to eat some crow.

I stepped out of my car and waved to Cody in what I hoped was a friendly manner. To my great relief, he smiled and walked over.

"I wanted to apologize for last week," I said.

"So did I," he said. "And to give you this." He handed me a card.

Confused, I tore open the envelope. Inside was a condolence card signed by many people. Cody's name was the largest, under the printed message.

"Everyone in the office singed it," he explained. "It was extreme bad luck to lose your first cria that way. We all felt bad for you."

I bit my lip and closed the card. "I feel like such a heel for throwing you out that night."

"Oh, I understand," he said. "Worse things have happened when I gave bad news. At least you didn't throw anything or threaten to sue."

I sniffed and hoped I wouldn't tear up. "Did you come all this way to give this to me?"

"I was scheduled to check on Missy, but since I was coming this way…" He shrugged.

"Oh. Missy's doing great," I said. "Want to see her?"

"Sure," Cody said. "Don't you, um, want to change first?"

I looked down at my lavender skirt-suit and white blouse. "I suppose I've ruined enough office clothes for one month." Over his shoulder, I saw Lew ambling over to us. I imagined the conversation they were going to have, and my cheeks burned. I went inside and changed into my barn clothes as quickly as I could.

They weren't outside when I came back out, so I headed to the barn where Missy and the other alpacas were. When I stepped into the barn, Cody and Lew looked up at me, Cody with a guilty look, and Lew, as always, grinning.

I smiled. "How's our girl look today?"

"Fine, fine, just fine," Lew said. "Don't you think so, Dr. Arden?"

Cody looked away. Was he blushing? "She looks great from here," he said. "I'll have to get my hands on her to tell for sure."

Lew chuckled, and I looked at him. I had the feeling that someone was being teased, but I couldn't tell if it was Cody or me. "So let's catch her and see," I said.

Cody hung back and watched as Lew and I cornered Missy. Lew took her neck and I took hold of Missy's back end. Then I looked up and found Cody watching me. My heart flipped at the way his eyes held mine, and I forgot to breathe for a moment. He stepped into the stall and came closer, moving slowly, but not taking his eyes off of me. Finally, he was so close, I could have reached out and touched him, but before I did—and I might have—he dropped to one knee and began working on Missy's leg.

I stared at the top of his head, at his mop of tousled black curls, and wondered what that look meant. I let the alpaca's fleece slide through my fingers and wondered if Cody's black hair was as soft as hers.

I heard a little sound to my right and looked at Lew. I had forgotten he was in the stall. His ubiquitous smile was wistful.

Cody sat back on his heels and smiled at us. "This looks great," he said to me. "She doesn't need the bandage anymore. That was some fine nursing, Meg."

I smiled at him, still feeling a bit undone. I let Missy go and ran a hand through my own curls. "Lew and Molly were the real pros here," I said. "Missy will be okay?"

"Yes. She's a trooper," he said. "That leg will heal up perfectly. The hair will grow back a little more slowly, but give it time."

"Pooh. I don't care about the hair on her feet," I said.

Missy came up for a neck rub, so I scratched her. She leaned into my hand and hummed at me.

"Well, then." Cody stooped to gather his things. "I'll send you a bill at the end of the month."

"I'll walk you out," I volunteered.

I walked past a suddenly silent Lew and a surprised-looking Cody and held the stall door for the vet. Then I walked beside him to his truck. I didn't know what I was doing, but something in Cody's eyes had whispered to me.

"I just wanted to apologize, again, for that night last week," I said again.

"Think nothing of it."

"No, really." I took a breath and laid a hand on his arm. "I am really sorry. I shouldn't have blamed you for making that hard decision in my…absence." I looked into his eyes. "I was caught off guard. And I blamed you when I shouldn't have."

Cody looked down and put his hand over mine for a moment, then drew away. "You're forgiven."

"Oh, okay. Well, s—see you later, t—then," I stammered like an idiot. "I'll just go in until chores."

He smiled and turned to go.

What the hell? Don't let him go!

"Wait!" I said. "Do you want a cup of coffee?"

Cody paused with his hand on the door of his truck. When he looked up at me, my heart ached. "Not today," he said. "I've got to go back to the clinic."

"Well, thanks again for the card," I said.

"You're welcome."

He climbed into the cab of his truck and started the engine. Then he waved and smiled and pulled out of my driveway. I heard him turn on the radio full blast, and he drove away from my house like a bat out of hell. I hated to think what Lew had said to change the look in those brown eyes. I had my suspicions, though.

⚘⚘⚘

This is a very, very bad idea.

My brain was chanting, yelling at me as I stood on the mounting block next to Albert, a huge, yellow, benign beast who now turned his head to see what was taking me so long. I had spent my Sunday morning following Rosie around, first petting horse noses, and then stepping into the stalls to rub horse necks, finally to this point, about to mount a horse for the first time in years.

I kept trying to picture myself getting on Billingham or Buster when I was younger. It was so easy! Just swing your leg over the saddle. *It's the farthest you can get from the feet*, I kept telling myself.

Very, very bad idea.

I grasped the pommel on Albert's saddle, trying not to hyperventilate.

"Meg?" Rosie stood at my hip. "You okay?"

"Yeah, yeah. I can do this."

"You know Albert will take care of you, right? He's my best school horse. I put four-year-olds on him."

But he's still got huge, hard feet!

"Shut up," I muttered and swung my leg over the saddle. The old palomino sighed as I settled my weight onto his back, and he swished his tail critically. "I'm not that heavy," I said.

Rosie laughed. "He's used to carrying wispy pre-teen girls," she said. "I'm sure it wasn't personal." She put her hand on my knee. "You okay up there? You're breathing kind of fast."

"Yeah." I closed my eyes and focused on not panting by counting to five between breaths.

"Good." Rosie squeezed my calf. "So, this should be

just like riding a bicycle. Show me what you remember."

I gathered the reins in my hands and squeezed my legs into Albert's sides. He twitched his ears at me.

Oh, no. Now what?

"He's a school horse," Rosie said. "Be more firm with him. Click."

I tried again, digging my heels deeper into his yellow hide and clicking my tongue. This time, Albert stepped forward into a walk, dropping his head, and swinging those great feet so they kicked up clods of soft dirt from the arena floor.

"Nice!" Rosie called. "Don't look at the ground. Just get to know each other for now. Do a couple of turns or something."

Albert and I did a turn around the arena at a walk that was closer to a plod, and I willed my hands not to shake. Then I turned him around and went in the other direction.

I didn't need Rosie to tell me that I was stiff in the saddle or that my feet weren't in the right position. But I didn't want to try to change anything, yet. I just sat in the saddle and tried not to think about how big Albert was or how his scent reminded me of that day fifteen years ago when I was lying in unconscious in a half-mucked stall with a crazed horse who was trying to kill a rake five feet from me.

I took another deep breath. *Albert is not dangerous*, I told myself. In fact, when I opened my eyes, I saw that Albert had carefully stepped around a low beam that I had been inadvertently steering toward. I leaned forward to rub his mane, and he swung his head up some so he could smile at me with his eye.

An hour later, Albert and I were trotting happily around the arena. Rosie wasn't quite right: getting back up on a horse isn't exactly like getting back on a bicycle, but I did remember lots more than I had expected to. I dismounted smiling and pulled off my helmet. "That was great!"

"Awesome," Rosie said. "You didn't look afraid at all out there."

"I was terrified at the beginning, Rosie. Even Albert knew that."

"Of course. Albert's a pro."

"Can I come back?"

"Sure," said Rosie.

"How much do I owe you?"

She waved my offer away. "Friends' money is no good here," she said. "If you get serious and want lessons, we'll talk. If you just want to have some fun, I should be able to find a horse that needs a little exercise or a trail ride."

"Trail ride?"

"Don't worry," she said, patting my shoulder. "We'll work up to it."

Putting Albert away was a challenging because I needed to actually touch his feet to pick them clean. It didn't help that the big blond gelding was part draft horse, so his feet were the size of dinner plates. But he waited patiently, turning his head in the crossties to see why I was just hovering around his front foot, panting.

"Shall I?" Rosie asked. Grateful, I nodded and handed her the hoof pick. She lifted each of Albert's feet and flicked out the mud from the many crevasses. "Don't worry," she said when she was done. "You'll get there. Let's go inside for some coffee."

Rosie's house was a new manufactured home. When I drove up earlier that morning, I wondered why anyone would buy a trailer to live in, but I was very surprised at the interior of the place, which was roomy and airy. I'd expected a close, dark place that was cramped, like Lew and Molly's ancient trailer. However, Rosie, despite her horse-themed furnishings, was a tidy housekeeper and, except for the mudroom, which housed the barn clothes and muddy boots, the place sparkled. I think her place was even larger than mine.

I sat at the kitchen bar next to a sculpture of a horse head as Rosie poured the coffee. "I like your place," I said.

"Thanks." Rosie sat next to me and looked around. "My first place here burned five years ago, just after Bill died. This was easier than living with Dad and Molly for ten months while a contractor got around to rebuilding. I think it came out nice."

"Is the resale as bad as they say?" I asked in financial-planner mode.

Rosie shrugged. "I never really considered resale," she admitted. "Frankly, when you don't plan on leaving until they have to carry you out in a box, resale value doesn't really come into the question."

"Point taken," I said, smiling and thinking of Nana.

"So, I hear Cody Arden was at your place again this week."

I made a face. "You want to talk about *men*?"

"I hear he thinks you're cute," Rosie continued and took a sip of coffee, her eyes laughing at me over the brim. She was so Lew's daughter.

"Really?" I frowned. "He was in such a hurry to get away from me, I was sure he thought I was hideous."

"That might have something to do with Evan," Rosie said.

"How does he know about Evan?" I asked. "Oh, wait. Everybody knows about Evan."

"My father is an awful gossip," Rosie said.

"So Cody avoids me because I've gone out with Evan."

Rosie tilted her head. "Gone out with? Is that what you kids are calling it these days?"

"Right," I said, nodding. "Everyone knows about the Sunday brunch in the Saturday night dress, too. Forgot about that."

"So, are you serious about Evan?" Rosie was persistent, I'd give her that. "Please tell an old widow so she can live vicariously through you."

I had to laugh. "Old?"

"Okay. Still. Widow," she said, pointing to herself. "Dating," she said, pointing to me.

I shrugged. "We've gone out a few times now. I really like him…"

"I hear a 'but' in the air."

"But I think my boss is in love with him and is punishing me for dating him by heaping shit work on me."

"Ugh."

"And…"

"And?"

"And Evan doesn't really like animals. Never had a pet."

"Really?" Rosie leaned against the counter and cocked her head. "Do you think that will be a problem?"

"You know, he asked the same thing." I watched the steam rise from my cup. "Right now, a couple weeks in, it's not a problem. Later, it might be. We'll see."

Rosie looked thoughtful. Then she smiled, but didn't say anything.

"What about you?" I asked. "Why aren't you dating?"

Rosie sighed. "Bill wasn't the perfect man," she said. "But being with him was effortless. Nothing about dating now is effortless."

"Everything about dating is effort," I agreed. "It was hard when I was young, but now, everything is either too complicated, or not complicated at all."

"What do you mean?"

I rolled my eyes. "Let's just say that I stopped dating because of too much effortless dating and not enough 're-al' dating."

She nodded. "Got off the lead and ran wild, did you?"

I smiled. "I suppose that's one way to look at it. Whatever it was, it wasn't productive." I stared at the horse head next to me. "You have to watch out for men in their thirties. They're either divorced, or bachelors, or married, which are all red flags in my book. In Berkeley, I was seeing the worst kinds of all three types."

"Isn't Evan divorced?"

"Yeah," I said. "And I actually don't know that story. He says he would rather not talk about exes at the start of a relationship."

"Doesn't that strike you as odd?"

"Now that you mention it, yes. Do you know anything about it?"

She hesitated a moment before shaking her head. "His wife left him pretty soon after they arrived here. The scuttlebutt is that she didn't like small town living, but he does."

"I found my husband in the shower with the foreign college student we paid to clean the house," I told her. "Somehow a difference in opinion about the town you live in doesn't sound that bad." I drained my cup. "I think I need to go home and take a long bath, or I'll be sore tomorrow."

"You'll be sore, anyway," said Rosie. "But far be it for me to keep a girl from a tub of hot water."

As I drove home through the woods and pastures that undulated around my new home, I thought about the end of relationships. Beth, in the throes of a badly ending "thing," had once sobbed into my shoulder, "Why do we do it, Meg? Why do we even start? Unless you're both killed in the same car crash, one of you is going to leave the other one alone. If all relationships end, why even start one?"

At the time, all I could do was stammer something about how silly Beth was being because I didn't know the answer. Why did we put ourselves through it all if the end was going to be bad? My husband crushed my trust, Bill had died and left Rosie convinced no other man in the world was worth the effort, and Evan's wife had left because she didn't like their new address.

I sat in the car after I pulled into my driveway, watching the alpacas, my mind wandering to the future. How would it end with Evan? Would we get married? Would he move to my farm? Would I have to sell the farm to move into town with him? Would he cheat, too? Would he die? I was suddenly convinced that the little fucker would die first and leave me old and alone.

Then I remembered the feeling of Evan's hand on my face when he kissed me under the oak tree. Just as suddenly, I remembered the way I'd felt when Cody's brown eyes met mine.

For that matter, I remembered how Martin would bring me flowers for no reason at least twice a week. I used to smile at the sound of his voice singing as he washed the car on sunny Saturdays. We used to hold hands during summer open-air pops concerts sitting on a blanket in the grass.

I knew then why everyone started relationships, knowing they might end badly. The beginnings and middles of relationships could be so wonderful that they outweighed the possibility of a bad ending.

I wondered if Beth had ever figured that out.

Chapter 7

I was soaking my tired body in a bubble bath when my cell phone rang. Shaking one hand dry, I plucked the phone off the windowsill and, peeking at the screen, answered it with "Margot? Is it really you?"

"Meg!" she said. "How are things up there in the wilderness?"

"Things are…challenging, but good."

"Any mountain lions or mountain men we should know about?"

"Well, now that you mention it," I said, settling back into the warm water, careful not to get bubbles on my phone.

"Go on." I could picture Margot sitting forward on her chair at her tiny, plant-covered kitchen table. She was the only person I knew who still avoided cell phones and made calls from a landline in her kitchen. The phone even had a cord. "Do tell! I want to hear how the dating moratorium ended."

"Well—"

"No, wait! I have a better idea," she cried. "Tell me in person."

"Margot, I don't have time to make a trip to California," I said. "I only just started my job and I'm still getting the hang of things here on the ranch—"

"You've got a guest room, don't you?"

"Sort of," I said, thinking of the room where I had stashed all the boxes I didn't think I needed to unpack until later.

"Great! Beth and I are coming up for a visit next week. Isn't that exciting?"

I sat up so quickly that I sloshed a lot of water out of the tub. "Really? Oh, God, that will be great. I've missed you guys so much."

After much planning, I hung up the phone and, donning my PJs, went straight to the guest room.

It was a disaster. I had dubbed it the "default room" while the movers were here, so whenever I didn't know where something went, I sent it to my extra room. Boxes were piled three or four high.

I began clearing the room out. When I started to glaze over, I stumbled to bed. It was midnight.

The next day Molly suggested I use a corner of the barn for my boxes instead of a storage unit, which expedited things a little.

My biggest surprise was when Evan offered to help paint.

"Oh, yeah," he said. "I kinda dig painting. I feel all manly when I get latex in my hair."

He came over that Saturday. Spring was finally getting warm and gave us a sunny day after most of a week of overcast and rain. Evan took off his shirt after we spread the drop cloth, and I made a silent prayer of gratitude to the warm weather gods. With his help, the painting went so quickly that we were able to clean up before we made sandwiches for lunch. We put stuff back into the room after we ate. He never bothered to put his shirt back on.

Evan and I put together the bed frame in the newly robin's egg blue guest room. He was all too happy to help with that project, too. By the time we had strong-armed the box spring and mattress onto the frame, he was glowing deliciously.

We pushed the bed into position and then flopped onto it and sighed.

He turned his head to look at me. "That was fun."

"Sure was."

He reached over and tucked a curl behind my ear and laughed when it sprang back. "I love your hair."

"This mess? I've never been able to make it do anything!" That morning I had given up entirely and wrapped my head in a kerchief so I resembled a cleaning ad from the 1950s.

"Well, I love it," he said, and kissed the stray curl. Then he kissed my face, and then my lips.

He hovered over me a moment, and I smiled at him. "How did you get to be so sweet?" I asked.

"Multiple beatings as a child," he said, laughing. "How about you?"

"I decided to do the opposite of everything my ex has done to me," I said.

"Good plan," he said. "Here's to doing exactly the opposite of what our exes did. Starting here," and he leaned in and kissed me tenderly. "Is there anything I can do for you now, dear?"

"You can make love to me right now," I said. "Even though it's afternoon, and we're dirty, and only halfway done with the project."

"Done," he replied, but I didn't really hear it because he had buried his face in my neck.

✺

I wasn't sure why, but I refused Evan's offer to come with me to pick up my girlfriends at the airport. Some company would have been nice during the 90-minute drive to Portland, but I had to admit his presence would have hampered the discussion once my friends arrived. He was topic number one on the agenda, after all.

For some reason, I didn't want my friends to think I had changed since I left two months ago, so I carefully chose my outfit to reflect the warm weather and obligatory shopping trip to the outlet mall—made even better in this state with no sales tax.

When I turned around in front of the mirror that morning, I realized that I had worn the same breezy top, floaty skirt, and heels several times in Berkeley last summer—with the addition of a sweater to combat the chilly morning fog.

I also hit a car wash on the way to the airport to erase any evidence of the gravel road leading up to my house. The scratches were still there, but at least you could tell the color of the car.

Still, I was nervous as I waited for my friends outside of security. I knew they wouldn't judge me unfairly. They had no reason to. Still, I was jittery until I saw them emerging from the throng of passengers. Then I ran up and threw my arms around them. We squealed and bounced like teenagers, not like career women in their thirties.

"I can't believe it's only been two months," Beth cried as we dragged their luggage to my car. "You are so tan! Have you been hitting the beds?"

"Those things are so bad for you," Margot clucked.

"No, no," I said. "I've just been outside more."

"Outside?"

"You know, that place on the other side of your front door?" Margot said.

"But you're gardening all the time, and you're not that tan," Beth protested. "I'm sure she's got a tanning bed somewhere."

"I live in Berkeley," Margot reminded her. "We get a fraction of the sunshine that this place does. Am I right, Meg?"

"Less sunshine than *Oregon*?"

"Surprisingly, Margot's right," I said. "I haven't kept track or anything, but yeah. April was pretty soggy, but the sun would come out at least briefly every day. That's when I'd try to get out in the field and sit with the alpacas."

"Right, the alpacas," Beth said as she shut the back of my SUV. "How's that going?"

"Huge learning curve," I said. "But they are the most charming animals. Totally worth it."

"Are you going to make a business out of it?" Margot asked.

"Still the plan. I'm learning the ropes, though."

"And what about the mountain man you eluded to?" Margot said.

"Yes, where is he?"

I smiled and started the car. "I'll tell you about Evan on the way," I said. "For now, seatbelts on."

That evening, after we had cleaned out several shoe outlets, Evan met us at an airy restaurant for dinner. We arrived in a bubble of contented post-shopping chatter and heaved a collective sigh as we sat down at the table. Margot and Beth gave Evan an appraising look as he held my chair for me and kissed the top of my head. They both nodded discretely at me as he sat.

"We could have used you at the shops today, Evan," Margot said. "We needed a strong back to carry our plunder." Even though she was an avowed hippie chick, Margot loved designer clothes and could outlet-shop with the best of them. Even my mother had been impressed by Margot's shopping prowess.

"It is an impressive haul," I said. "You can't see out of the back of the car."

"Good thing I drove myself up," he said. "Doesn't sound like there'd be room for me at all."

"It might be a tight fit, but I'm sure we could find a place for you," Margot said. "You know, if necessary."

"Margot!" Beth knew, even if Evan didn't, that Margot's method of testing out our potential boyfriends was to liberally apply her earthy brand of flirtation. Beth didn't exactly approve of this tactic.

After the wine came and we ordered food, my friends and I went to the bathroom together, claiming that we hadn't been since the airport. Evan waved us goodbye. He knew what we were up to.

"Oh, my God, Meg. He's beautiful," Beth cried once the door was closed.

"I know," I said. "And I don't even like redheads."

"Is it all red?"

"Margot!"

I smiled and shrugged. "I don't kiss and tell."

"Oh, please," Margot rolled her eyes. "Like we came 500 miles not to hear the gory details."

"Do you really like him?" I asked.

"Of course we do," Beth said. "He's handsome, funny, charming, just like you said. He's perfect. Where did you find him?"

"Is he perfect?" Margot asked.

"Pretty much."

"But?"

"Well, three things," I said, gathering my nerve. "First, he won't talk about his ex."

"Not good," muttered Beth.

"Second, is the whole 'my boss is in love with my boyfriend and punishes me for it' that I told you about."

"Right, that sucks." Beth leaned against the sink and frowned. "What are you going to do about that one?"

"I'm not sure. Right now, I'm just trying to keep a low profile until I know where this thing with Evan is leading."

"What about number three?" asked Margot.

"He isn't really an animal person."

Margot bit her lip in thought. "That's a long-term issue, right?"

"I suppose so."

"You need to talk to him about his ex," she said. "That concerns me more than the other things. You can always find another job, but you should know how his other relationship ended before you go further."

"You mean I can't go on blindly trusting him anymore?"

Margot and Beth shook their heads.

"No matter how handsome," Beth said.

"You both always say exactly what I hope you won't say."

"But we're always right," said Margot.

And, dammit, they always were.

ငှာင

The evening ended back at my house with more wine and conversation. When they went to bed, my friends insisted that they were going to get up for morning chores since we got back to the ranch too late to see the alpacas. The girls retired before Evan went home, probably assuming that he and I would cuddle or something. Instead, I copped to having a headache and sent him away. I collapsed in bed after applying the college hangover cure again. Hell, one day it might work.

Margot and Beth had forgotten all about morning chores by 6:30 a.m. when I went to roust them out of bed.

"Really, Meg?" Beth whined. "I'm on vacation here!"

"Pshaw!" I said. "Put on your jeans." I laughed and shoved coffee at them.

When they emerged from the guest room, Margot asked, "So, where's Evan?"

"Oh, he went home."

"Did you have a fight after we went to bed?" Beth asked.

"Oh, no. He's just never spent the night here."

"Why not?"

"Well," I said slowly. "It's just not time yet."

"Why not?" This time, Margot asked.

"The house is a mess, he'd have to endure me getting up for chores, a million reasons." I knew I sounded lame as I spoke these words, and I couldn't meet their eyes.

Margot and Beth glanced at each other. "So, he's not a real boyfriend, yet, is he?" asked Margot.

I closed my flapping jaw and then nodded.

"If he stays the night here, he's part of her life here," Margot explained to Beth. "She's not ready for that commitment."

"Is he?" asked Beth.

I pursed my lips. "I don't know."

"Is there someone else?" Margot pressed.

"Nnnnoo."

"Who? Who is it?" Beth asked, leaning forward.

"Let's go to the barn," I cried, and marched to the back door. "Come on, girls. No more stalling."

But they were still asking, "Who? Who?" like a pair of owls when we got to the barn. But they stopped when confronted by the wall of cute staring at them over the stall doors. "Oh, they are so adorable!" Beth cried as I showed her how to feed them pellets out of her hand.

"They look wise," Margot mused. "These are old souls."

Lew and Molly exchanged glances.

"These are my friends from Berkeley," I said to start the introductions. "I don't think they've spent much time with alpacas."

"We met Secretariat and Seabiscuit before," Beth said, as if visiting my Nana's farm once was the equivalent to owning a ranch. Then she squealed in delight as a baby alpaca began nibbling on her sweatshirt. Margot whispered with another alpaca as the rest of us put out water and hay.

Molly and Lew shook their heads. "We thought you were a little nuts when you first got here," Lew said to me. "We've changed our opinion."

To my dismay, however, as the novelty of the animals wore off, my friends turned back to their real interest.

"Who's this other man?" Beth asked again as she fed a handful of fresh hay to a little brown cria.

"Other man?" Molly was suddenly curious.

"We met Evan last night," Margot said. "But we've determined through our specialized interrogation techniques that the reason he's never spent the night is because there's a dark horse on the horizon."

Lew leaned on his rake and pushed the bill of his cap up. "No kidding."

"You don't sound surprised," Margot observed.

"I'm not," he said.

"They don't know anything about my love-life," I insisted, but I felt myself blushing.

"What do you know?" Beth said, ignoring me.

Lew laughed. "All I can do is speak the truth. The vet has a crush on her."

"He does not," I protested like a pre-teen.

My friends ignored me. "Is he cute? Is he single? How do you know he likes her?"

Lew basked in the attention and smiled. "A man knows these things," he said. "Except for the cute part. Molly?"

"Finger-licking," Molly said, watching me squirm.

"It sounds like you've got a great pair lined up, Meg," Beth said. "No wonder you don't want to leave."

"If any of you breathe a word of this to anyone alive or dead, I'll string you up," I said.

Even though all four of them were grinning at my embarrassment, I actually felt comforted. Not only was it nice to have my old friends teasing me in a familiar way, but Molly and Lew were behaving as friends, too.

"I should swear off men again just to deny all of you something to talk about."

"That'll be the day," Margot said, slipping her arm around my waist.

∽∾∽

After chores and breakfast, Beth, Margot, and I carried our chairs and coffee into the pasture for some communing. Missy came right up and introduced herself to Beth and Margot and then cushed down next to me to chew some cud.

Secretariat and Seabiscuit stood in the boys' pasture, whining for some attention.

Beth sank back in the spring sunshine and sighed. "This is the kind of ranching I could get behind."

Margot nodded. "I can see why you like it out here. This place puts my tiny garden patch to shame."

"You've got a great garden," I said. "Plus, I have two employees who do most of the work. But I do love it out here. And I love these little guys." I dropped my hand to scratch Missy's back.

"I can see that." Beth looked around appreciatively. "So, you've got it pretty good here, then?"

"What do you mean?"

"Well, you've got all your critters and your ranch. You've got not one, but two men interested in you. And, you've got a good job. You're really set up."

"Not bad for two months," Margot said.

I shrugged, but I couldn't help but smile. "What can I say? When Karma is good, it's good."

"Don't get too smug," Margot warned. "Karma likes to bite smug people in the ass."

"Noted," I said, grinning even more.

We finished our coffee and then I took them on a four-star tour of the area. We saw the historic courthouse, the town fountain, the riverside park, and the vineyards. Margot and Beth made me promise to arrange for wine tastings the next time they came to visit.

When we were done, we met Evan at the Pie House for lunch.

"Did you girls have fun playing farmer?" Evan asked after we'd ordered.

"Oh, yes," Beth said. "Aside from the animals, I can't see why Meg likes it so much. I mean, it's work."

Evan laughed. "I'm sure it is. But Meg loves it."

"What do you think of her ranch?" Margot asked.

She was too far away for me to kick her under the table, so I glared at her, instead.

"Me?" Evan shrugged. "I've been there a couple times, but I'm not really an animal person, so I suppose it would just be work for me."

"Really?" Beth asked. "You don't like animals?"

"I've never really had much contact with them," he said. "No pets as a kid or anything. I had a plant once, but nothing with a pulse."

"But you like animals?" Margot pressed.

"I suppose," he said. He put an arm around my shoulders. "I know Meg is crazy for her alpacas."

Margot, as she often did, abruptly changed tactics. "Did your ex-wife like animals?"

I shot daggers at her with my eyes, but she ignored me.

"Not really," Evan said. His arm across stiffened my shoulders. "She was allergic to cats and dogs and didn't see the point of fish. At least we agreed on that."

"But not much else?"

I tried desperately to get the waitress's attention, hoping a round of coffee would change the subject, but she didn't look my way.

"My ex and I didn't agree on much, but geography was the main issue. She hated it here. She hates small towns and said she was bored."

"Maybe you should have bought her an alpaca farm," Beth said. Bless her for trying to lighten the mood. "She would have been too busy to be bored."

"I can honestly say that never crossed my mind."

"You know Meg caught her husband cheating on her," Margot said.

I dropped my spoon and stared at her.

"I hadn't heard that she'd caught them," Evan said. He squeezed my shoulder gently and looked me in the eye. "What was that like?"

"Awful."

"It was a college student," Beth volunteered, so I had to hate her, too. "They paid her to clean the house."

"Martin apparently was helping her do the shower."

"Do you still hate him?" Evan asked.

"No," I said. "I don't exactly wish him well, but

'hate' implies that I care enough to apply emotion to him. It has been two years."

"We hate him enough to cover her part, plus some," Margot said. "Between the two of us, Martin's got plenty of negative energy funneled his way."

Beth giggled. "Plus some magazine subscriptions he didn't know he signed up for."

"What are you two? Sixteen?" I laughed.

"We pretend to be adults," Margot whispered to Evan, winking.

When the check came, Evan snatched it and went to the cashiers to pay, leaving us to gossip.

"Well, the more I see him, the better I like him," Beth said.

"Me, too," Margot said.

"That's high praise from you, Earth-mother." I reached out to finish the last of my iced-tea when the bell at the front door jangled. My hand froze in the air. "Oh, God," I said. Cody had walked into the restaurant.

"What?" Beth swung around in her chair to follow my gaze. "Oh, my. He's cute."

"That's the vet, isn't it?" Margot whispered. I nodded. "Dear, pick up your glass."

As I followed Margot's direction, Cody caught sight of me and waved. Then he walked up to our table, and my heart stopped beating.

"Deep breaths," Margot whispered.

"Hello, Meg. Who are your friends?" Cody said, smiling warmly at us.

"Cody," I croaked. "These are my friends from

Berkeley, Margot and Beth." I watched as he shook their hands feeling a pang of envy that they got to touch him, and I did not. Then he stood awkwardly for a moment.

"How are things with the alpacas?" he said, as if he'd been trying to think of something to say.

"Oh, fine," I said. "They're good. I gave my friends the tour earlier today."

"Did she show off her bandaging work?"

"Why, no," Beth said.

"Missy, wasn't it? Got her foot caught in a fence the first week Meg was here."

"It was my first day of work, even," I said.

"Wow, really? Anyway, after some initial difficulty," Cody said with a wink that made my insides melt. "She learned to care for the wound. It healed faster than any I've seen. I was really proud of her stepping up like that." He was looking at me so warmly that I blushed and looked down at my empty plate.

"Stepping up to what?" Evan asked. He was smiling as he slid into the booth next to me, but he put his arm around my shoulders so firmly that I may have jumped a little.

"Uh, the way she bandaged a wound—on an alpaca," Cody said. His smile seemed firm as well.

"Evan, this is my vet, Dr. Cody Arden," I said as cheerfully as I could.

"Pleasure," Evan said, taking his arm off of my shoulders long enough to shake Cody's hand.

Brief though it was, each of us girls could feel the silent communication as the two men clasped hands and locked gazes. When the two-second handshake was over, Evan wrapped his arm around my waist, and Cody took a step back.

"Well, I'll let you get on with your day," he said. "I'm just picking up some lunch on my way to a farm call. Give me a ring if you need anything, Meg—you know, livestock-related."

"Sure. I will. Bye." I waved as he walked to the counter to pick up his food. When I turned back, I saw my two friends watching me carefully.

Evan looked at Cody a moment longer before he turned back to the table. "So, do you girls want to see the waterfalls or the beach today?"

"Beach," Margot said as Cody finished paying and caught my eye. He gave us a little wave and then left with his food.

‹›‹›

As soon as we stepped out of the car and the heavy smell of the ocean met me, I knew we were in the right place. I hadn't realized that I missed the salty air or the cry of seagulls until we got there and the wind whipped our hats off of our heads and filled our shoes with sand.

We walked down the steps from the parking lot to the beach and took our shoes off on the bottom step. The sun was veiled behind the thin clouds, but managed to warm the top layer of sand a little. I still snuggled into my jacket a little deeper to keep the wind out. But, like true north-coast residents, we kept our shoes off even when the cold ocean turned our toes purply-pink. The cool coast in Oregon was very much like the beaches in the Bay Area, and we had fun beachcombing and not talking about Cody Arden.

It was very nice to hang on Evan's arm as a pair of wet dogs danced around us and my friends chattered like seabirds. I was content and forgot meeting Cody at lunch. Well, at least I tried to be content and forget about meeting Cody at lunch.

However, after we drove back to town and dropped Evan off at his apartment, Beth and Margot began grilling me, as expected.

"*That* was the vet?" Beth started when we got out of Evan's driveway. "I pictured some old guy in a white coat who smelled like cat pee. My God. If you don't want him, send him my way!"

"Seems shy," Margot observed.

"Evan's no slouch, but what made you pick him?" Beth asked.

"He asked," I said. "Plus, I was really angry at Cody for a while. A baby alpaca died, and I blamed him."

"Oh yeah," Margot said. "I remember. You almost came home."

"It wasn't Cody's fault, but I said some things. I am actually surprised he still talks to me."

"Honey, it's pretty obvious he wants to do more than talk."

"Evan knows it, too. Did you see the way he was marking his territory?" Beth said from the back seat.

"You might want to watch that," Margot said. "I had

a boyfriend who was possessive. It didn't end well."

"It's not like that," I said, gripping the steering wheel tighter.

Margot arched an eyebrow from the passenger seat "Oh? What is it like?"

"The hell if I know," I cried. "I know Evan likes me because he's told me so. I only have a rumor that Cody 'thinks I'm cute.' I have no fucking idea what is actually going on, and I am tired of being second-guessed by everyone I meet."

I hit the gravel road to my house faster than usual, and the BMW fishtailed wildly. I hit the gas and powered through it, not caring about possible mailbox causalities. By the time we pulled onto the concrete pad in front of my garage, we were all quiet, but unscathed. I turned off the motor, and we listened to it click for a few moments.

"We're sorry, Meg," Beth ventured.

"No, I'm sorry," I said. "I get angry when I get embarrassed. I'm not mad at you. I don't know who I'm mad at. Probably myself."

"What for?" Margot asked.

I shook my head. "Fuck if I know."

&

The next morning, I couldn't get Beth or Margot out of bed, so I did chores without them. Lew didn't bring up the lunchtime meeting of Evan and Cody, so maybe he hadn't heard. I hoped that the event had gone unnoticed by the rest of the town, too, but I'd soon know.

Lew had better connections than a LA gossip columnist.

When I got back in from the barn, I found my friends happily drinking coffee and chatting at my kitchen table. "Morning," I called as I kicked off my barn shoes in the mudroom. "How'd you guys sleep?"

"Fine," Beth said. "So, you're not mad at us?"

"No," I said, pouring myself a cup and plunking into a chair at the table. "I was pissed last night because, well, I was embarrassed. Don't you just hate it when you revert to a teenager?"

"Sure," Margot said. "Some days I forget I'm a thirty-something."

"Isn't dating supposed to get easier as you get older?" I asked.

"You'd think," Beth said. "Maybe our emotions don't actually get older."

Margot laughed. "If only our bodies had stopped at seventeen, too."

"So, are the boys topic *verboten*?" Beth asked.

"No," I said. "Just don't expect any surprising developments. And please don't try to help."

A little later, Lew knocked loudly on the door as Beth, Margot, and I were finishing our bagels. "Hey, Meg. We've got a lady in labor out here. Wanna see?"

"Oh! Is she all right?" I asked.

Lew nodded. "Yes, she's fine. Ought to be a good one."

As I headed for the door, Margot called, "Wait for us!"

The barn was lighter than it had been earlier during chores, so it was easier to see the alpaca in labor. It was Isabelle, a brown beauty with an extremely fluffy topknot and fleece down to her toes. Lew and Molly had already shooed her back into the barn so they could keep an eye on her, so the three of us sat on a bale of hay to watch. When Belle turned around in the stall, Beth squealed, "Look! Feet!"

I wished I had brought a camera because the look on Beth and Margot's faces was priceless: that mix of fascination and horror usually reserved for car accidents and train wrecks.

"Shh! That's what supposed to come out first," I said.

As we watched, the little brown feet and legs pushed farther and farther out until we also saw a little black nose. I wondered if Beth was going to make it without barfing.

"Won't be long now," Molly said.

"Come on, Mama," Lew said. "Keep pushing."

Suddenly, there were eyes and ears that blinked and twitched at us.

"Omigod!" Beth wiggled. "That's so amazing."

All at once, the baby plopped out, landing in a heap on the ground.

"Is it all right?" cried my stoic friend, Margot, leaping to her feet. "Wasn't Mama supposed to lie down?"

"Nope, this was text-book perfect," Molly said, grabbing a towel. "Come on, Meg. This is the fun part."

Molly, Lew, and I stepped into the stall to dry off the

baby and dip its belly button in iodine to prevent infec-
tion. The baby's snake-like neck wobbled up from the
ground. Belle sniffed and sniffed it, humming the whole
time.

"Why are you drying it with towels?" Margot asked
at one point.

Lew looked up. "To dry it quickly so it won't get too
chilled. It's a little cold this morning."

"Is it okay?" I asked Lew quietly as we worked next
to each other.

"It seems just fine," he said, looking at me. "You
don't need to worry."

Then, as we stepped back, Molly checked under the
tail.

"Congratulations," she said. "It's a girl."

"Oh," Beth cooed. "What are you going to name
her?"

"How about 'Rachel Alexandra' after the filly that
won the Kentucky Derby?" Margot suggested.

"That sounds perfect," I said, smiling at the tiny
creature.

We went back to the bale to watch for another hour
as little Rachel Alexandra took command of her freakish-
ly long legs and neck. She was standing within forty
minutes. She was trying to nurse in forty-five. That's
when Lew opened the stall door and let them outside.

"You don't think it's too soon?" I asked.

"No, it's good for them to get moving. Isabelle is an
experienced mom, and she knows to go slowly and to
stand still while the baby nurses. These two will be better

off with the herd. Mama will get anxious if she's separated from her friends for too long."

"We know how that is," Margot said, smiling at me.

We watched the new pair as they entered the herd, and I saw for the first time the ritual greeting of baby alpacas into the herd: each animal went up to the baby, head down, ears erect, and sniffed Rachel all over, from head to foot. She stood with her head high, ears back, and tiny tail curled over her back, which Molly said meant, "I'm just a baby! Don't hurt me!"

I kept watching the new little one from my window as my friends packed up for home. Lew had called Cody to come and check the baby out, but the vet would arrive while I was on my way to drop my friends off at the airport. I wasn't sure if I was relieved that I would miss him or disappointed.

Chapter 8

I recognized Martin's handwriting on the envelope immediately and stood holding the letter for a long moment. I'd picked up the mail on my way home from dropping the girls off at the airport, but I hadn't noticed his letter until later that evening when I sorted it. Curiously, he had only written my name. My address was in a hand I didn't know at all. My first impulse was to throw the letter out, and I held the envelope at arm's length over the paper recycle bin, letting it dangle from my fingertips, but I couldn't let it go. Finally, I sat down at the kitchen table and tore open the end, peeking in just in case there was some white powder.

Inside was a single sheet of notebook paper, ragged edges still attached, a pet peeve of mine. Martin's close, precise engineering handwriting was looser and more jagged than usual, which alarmed me.

Meg,

You won't answer my emails, you moved away, and your bitchy lawyer and your equally bitchy friends won't give me your new address. I bribed the secretary at the law firm to mail this for me. I hope I didn't just waste $100.

You might have heard that Nadja left me. She found some teenager in college with a trust fund and a fast car and was gone like smoke. Little gold-digging cunt.

This is the fifth time I've started this letter, and I've decided, in the spirit of brevity, to just come out and say this: You were the best thing that ever happened to me. I'm sorry I fucked up. Please call me. I want to make this right.

Love you always,
Martin

I sat, numb, for I don't know how long, staring at Martin's signature. Then I re-read the letter. Then I read it again.

Finally, I called Margot. I broke into tears when she answered. "Oh, my God!" Margot said when she heard me crying on the other end of the phone. "Did someone die?"

"No!" I wailed.

"Meg? I just got home from the airport. What happened?"

When I could speak without too much hiccupping, I read the letter to her.

"Wow," Margot said after a moment. "I had no idea he thought I was bitchy. No, wait. I did know that." She chuckled.

"I don't see anything funny about this," I said.

"I'm sorry," Margot said. "I'm just a sucker for a comeuppance story. Please, go on." I could hear her trying to stifle sniggers.

"I almost didn't open it," I said. "Just seeing my name written in his handwriting made me mad."

"Why?"

"He wrote 'Megan Hunter.'"

Margot burst out laughing again. "He doesn't even know you've changed back to your maiden name?"

"Apparently not."

She giggled again. "So, how do you feel?"

"What do you mean?"

"Well, Martin's chica cheated on him and left."

"And?"

"Doesn't that make you just a little happy? Aren't you grinning just a little bit?"

"Well. Now that you mention it." I smiled. It felt good.

"Isn't it just a little funny?"

A giggle bubbled up and I laughed. "Isn't there a German word for enjoying someone else's suffering?"

"*Schadenfreude*. See, Mom and Dad? My German major saves the day again!" she cried.

I laughed.

"Seriously," she said when we'd calmed a bit. "I would have thrown his letter away. Why'd you open it?"

"Curiosity?" I said.

"What kind of curiosity?" Margot asked. "The, 'what on earth can he want?' kind or the 'what if?' kind?"

"I don't know," I said. "Maybe a little of each."

"I've talked you off this cliff before, Meg," my friend said. "We know what kind of man Martin is, right?"

"The lying, cheating, he-always-comes-first kind." I chanted the mantra Beth and Margot had drilled into me right after Martin left.

"Right. Those things are true. We didn't just make them up to make you feel better. Beth and I could tell right from the beginning he was always going to be first."

"Why didn't you say anything?"

"I believe we did," Margot said. "But talking to you when you think you're in love is like talking to a brick wall. You know that about yourself, right? Completely un-convincible when you're smitten."

"I know," I said. "What about the other things? Did you know he was a liar and a cheat before I did, too?"

"No, we all sort of found that out together, didn't we?"

We sat quietly for a moment.

"So what do I do about the letter?"

"Honestly, the best thing for you to do is throw it away."

"Really? What if—"

"I knew there was a 'what if' in there," Margot said. "Listen. He hasn't changed. If you go back to him, things will probably not be different."

"Probably?"

"Meg, do you like your life up there?"

I paused. "Yes, I do."

"And you like the man you're with? Or should I say 'men'?"

I smiled. "I see your point."

"Martin won't like any of those things. You'll have to move back here, give up the alpacas, your new job. You'll be 'Mrs. Hunter,' again."

I felt a cold shiver run over my skin.

"Throw it away. Shred it and put it in your compost pile. The fresh stuff, so you won't be tempted in a moment of weakness."

"Okay," I said.

"We're all tempted by the phantom ex, honey," Margot said. "In our lonely moments, we tend to remember only the good, rosy times and forget all the bullshit. Your friends won't forget the bullshit, though. That's what we're here for."

After I hung up, I dialed Beth's number and read her the letter, too. I explained Margot's suggestion and laughed.

"I have to admit, I'm looking forward to burying his words in manure," I said.

"I hate to say this, but I don't agree," Beth said.

"You don't? Why not?"

"Meg, you are always taking the simplest way out of these kinds of things. I mean, you haven't even spoken to Martin since—the incident, right?"

"No. Why would I speak to the little shit?"

"Well, you're still angry about it for one thing," she said. "Without confronting him, you are going to have trouble moving on. I'm not advocating you go back to him, not at all. Margot is spot on with that. But, well, without telling him what he's done to you and expressing the pain you feel and stuff, he's always going to be there, you know? There."

"That's not true," I said. "I hardly ever think of him anymore."

"Liar," Beth said.

Beth's forcefulness surprised me. "What makes you think I'm lying?"

"The fact that this letter made you so upset. That tells me that Martin is just under the surface. Plus, you told Margot that you did wonder 'what if.' That's what you said, right?"

"'Yeah." I thought for a moment. "So, you want me to write him back?"

"Yes. Send it to me and I'll mail it to keep him from tracking you down. Tell him what a fuck job he is."

"Fuck job, Beth?"

"He still makes me angry," Beth said.

I could imagine her sitting in a pretty flowered dress, pouting like a three-year-old.

"I'll think about it," I said.

"You do that," Beth said. "It would be good for you, Meg. You need to confront life more and accept it less."

I hung up the phone and stared at the letter lying in front of me. The easiest way to deal with it was to follow Margot's advice and destroy it. Let Martin stew in his own juices waiting for a reply. What right did he have writing me in the first place? The best place in the world for that piece of paper was under a steaming pile of alpaca poo. *Mrs. Hunter, indeed!*

I plucked up the letter, intending to march out to the manure pile, but instead I re-read it standing at my kitchen table. I read each word in time to the beating of my heart, and my pulse increased with each line until I had to sit down again. Beth was right: the son-of-a-bitch was still under my skin.

I flipped Martin's letter over and began writing on the back of the lined notebook paper in angry little letters.

> *Dear Son of a Bitch,*
>
> *How dare you write me? It's bad enough that you think you have a right to after the way you treated me, but to ask me to come back? What the hell did you think was going to happen?*
>
> *In case you forgot, you cheated on me, in my house, breaking our wedding vows. You shattered my trust in men. It's taken me this long to surround myself with people I can trust, and I'm not going to let you destroy that. This door is closed, mister, and you're the one who threw the key off of the cliff. You may not contact me again. I won't make the mistake of opening a letter from you twice.*
>
> *You may go rot in hell.*
> *Megan Taylor*

I read my letter over and over again, feeling better each time. Soon, I was leaning back in my chair, laughing. I imagined Martin's reaction to receiving the envelope and then to reading the actual letter. I wished I could see the look on his face when he read the salutation.

Then I considered which would be worse—getting this letter in the mail, or waiting around for eternity. Which would be the crueler torture? Writing the letter was certainly cathartic. I felt much better for having expressed myself. Would reading it be cathartic for Martin, too? Did I want him to confront the asshole that he was and is, deal with it, and move on? Or did I want him to suffer, stagnate, and stew without knowing what my reaction to his words was? I thought about all the nights I had sat beside the phone waiting for a boy to call me. I thought about a short story Poe wrote where a man was walled up in a crypt without knowing why.

I decided that's exactly the way I wanted Martin to feel.

I stood up and crammed the letter into my back pocket. I stuffed my feet into my cute barn boots, grabbed a shovel, and marched to the manure pile. After digging a deep hole in the freshest pile, I took out the double-sided letter and tore it into little tiny pieces, which I let drift into the pit like snow, or stardust, or faded memories, or whatever melodramatic metaphor I could think of.

Then I scooped up pile after pile of steaming, drippy alpaca poop and filled the hole.

I felt so light afterward, I wanted to skip on the rooftop. I settled for drinking half a bottle of pinot noir while re-reading my favorite scary novel until midnight, then sinking into the best sleep I'd had in weeks.

えへんへん

Shit-work notwithstanding, the next day was a good day. Lunch with Evan was fun as always, and I made good headway through my toughest cases. Plus, I looked forward to playing with a baby cria when I got home. Little Rachel had dried off to be a gorgeous curly brown bombshell, and I couldn't wait to get my hands on her again. I left work in a buoyant mood, practically singing, "Have a good night, Nancy!" as I flounced out of the front door.

I was surprised when I got home to find Molly loading Lew into their truck. "Hey," I called, as I climbed out of my car. "What's up?"

"Lew's having a bit of indigestion," Molly said, her eyes belying her fear. "Nurse on the phone said to bring him in to the ER so the doc could look at him."

"Are you all right?" I asked Lew, grabbing his elbow to help him into the truck. His face was white and his breath came shallow and fast.

"Oh, fine. Molly just needs to learn to cook," he said, flashing a weak smile at me.

Molly closed his door and I touched her arm. "Do you want me to come with you?"

"No, no," she said. "He's just got some stomach pains. They come and go. Besides, the vet is coming, and someone needs to be here."

"Cody? He came when I took my friends to the airport."

She shook her head. "An emergency came up, so we rescheduled. But the baby needs a shot or two in the first twenty-four hours. No biggie. I'll give you a call if we—if I need to."

She started the truck and drove away. Lew managed a small wave, but when they were a ways down the drive, I thought I saw him crumple a bit against the door. I was worried and antsy, so I went inside and changed into my barn clothes. By the time I got back to the barn, I had convinced myself to follow Lew and Molly as soon as the vet left. I didn't like it when my friends made after-hours visits to the Emergency Room, and I especially didn't like it when I wasn't there with them.

Worried, I stepped into the barnyard and saw the little black and brown baby playing in the short spring weeds. Molly or Lew had closed Mama Isabelle and wee Rachel Alexandra with a few other alpacas in the barnyard so the vet didn't have to chase them all over the pastures. I let myself into the enclosure and flipped over an empty bucket to sit on. Missy ambled over, gave me a head-to-toe sniff, and allowed me to scratch her neck a little. As I did, the other alpacas crept toward me, including Belle and her baby. Once Belle was satisfied I wasn't a threat, she moved off to nibble on the brave new grass that was trying to colonize the barnyard.

Rachel Alexandra hung back and looked at me carefully. I adored the way baby alpacas look. Their eyes were so huge and Rachel's were framed by ridiculously long lashes. Her petite black nose quivered below her round head. She stretched her neck out and sniffed me as I held perfectly still. She blinked and shook her head, snorting, as if I didn't smell right, but then she stepped closer and sniffed again.

I was grinning like a fool. This time, I raised my hand so the baby could sniff my fingers. She took one snort and then sprang sideways, apparently just for the joy of it.

I laughed. "We'll have to nickname you 'Spring!'"

"That sounds like a good name," agreed a voice behind me.

I spun around so fast that I fell off my bucket and scattered the alpacas. I found myself on my butt in the barnyard, once again, facing Cody who was leaning against the fence. "How did you sneak up on me?" I asked.

He shrugged. "I think I got here while you were in the house. I was drawing up the vaccines when you walked by. I thought you weren't speaking to me or something because of your boyfriend in the restaurant, so I didn't say anything."

I stood and brushed off my bottom. "He's not my boyfriend. I just didn't see you." I tried to see if there was more mud on my pants.

"There's a little more just, ah, down a little," Cody said, but then he gave up and just let himself into the yard. He looked around. "Where are Lew and Molly?"

I frowned. "ER. Lew has indigestion or something."

"Oh." Cody looked more worried than his remark

suggested, but then he said, "Let's shoo them into the barn so we can catch them more easily."

I slid the barn door shut when only Belle and Springy Rachel were in the stall. The other doors were open, though, which cast plenty of sunlight into the space. It smelled of hay and… well, manure, but I realized that I was beginning to like the smell of fresh alpaca beans. They smelled like home, now.

"What are you smiling about?" Cody asked, smiling himself.

I jumped a little. How did I manage to forget that he was standing there? "I'm just thinking how much this place is beginning to feel like home," I said. Why not be honest?

Cody nodded. "I love barns. I have always felt at home in barns." He looked around and sighed. "It's probably the animals," he said. "They don't have these complicated worries. Their lives are pretty straightforward. The fact that they trust us is a miracle." He met my eyes. "Do you know what I mean?"

I nodded. Then I remembered to breathe.

Cody turned to the alpacas, which stood watching us from a corner. "Move slow, so we can catch them without terrifying the baby."

Even moving slowly, Rachel still struggled when Cody caught her up in his arms. Her little legs flailed and she hummed worriedly. Belle came up to them, humming and nosing her baby, until she was satisfied that Rachel wasn't hurt. Then the mama went to the hay bin and started eating.

"Here, hold this," Cody said, and handed me the leggy little bundle.

From this position, I could look Rachel Alexandra directly in the eye. They were so black that it was difficult to see the horizontal slit that was her pupil. Her eyes were large and mysterious. She hummed and then sniffed my face, which made me laugh.

"She likes you," Cody said, putting on his stethoscope.

He moved one of my hands so he could listen to the baby's chest and belly. His fingers left little electric pulses. I watched him work, seeing mostly the top of his head as he listened, but I also got to examine his face in profile and staring off into the distance as he felt the baby. His eyes were an even prettier brown than I remembered, and he had a stalk of hay in his dark hair. I hoped he couldn't hear my heart thumping in his stethoscope, too.

Finally, he drew a little blood and gave the baby her vaccines. "All done," he said. "She looks great."

He was done so quickly that I didn't want to stop holding her. I carried her over to her mother and set her on the ground. Rachel immediately ducked her head under her mom and began to nurse. I leaned against the wall of the barn. "That's what you mean about trust, right?" I said. "Belle knows we're here to help. It is a miracle, isn't it?"

"Yes, it is." Cody's voice was in my ear, so when I turned to him, we were face-to-face.

My heart raced again, and I held my breath. Cody put one hand on my shoulder and pressed me into the barn wall. He traced my jaw with his other hand, watching his fingers until they reached the point of my chin. Then he leaned in and kissed me softly.

The feeling of his lips on mine made my eyes close, and all my thoughts dissolved. I lifted a hand and closed it around the nape of his neck, twining my fingers in his hair. He pulled me closer and kissed me again, not so gently this time. I wasn't gentle, either. I think my leg may have wrapped itself around his leg, in fact. Finally, we pulled back and looked into each other's faces, but before we could say anything, Molly and Lew's truck tires crunched the gravel in the drive in front of their trailer. How the heck did they get back from the freaking emergency room so soon? I turned my head to look out the door of the barn, and Cody let me go, taking a big step back. I stood alone next to the barn wall, looking from him to the truck to him again.

"Go see how he is," Cody said, waving me away.

My insides dropped. Was he giving me permission to go, or was he dismissing me? I went on automatic pilot and walked out of the barn, but I stood a moment blinking in the bright light.

That's how I heard him say to himself, "I just wanted to try that once."

"Meg? Meg, can you help me get Lew out of the truck?"

Molly was struggling with Lew's long, lean limbs, so I leapt to her rescue. When Lew was out of the truck, I looked over my shoulder to see Cody letting the alpacas out of the barn into the warming sunshine.

❦❦❦

"…so they think the food poisoning is from the taco truck next to the drugstore. Lots of people have been coming in with similar symptoms," Molly explained as we settled Lew into his easy chair in the dark front room of the trailer. There was a large flowering bush blocking the front window, so I couldn't see if Cody was still outside.

I shook my head and tried to focus on Lew, who was still in pain, but not as gray or drawn as when he left. I knelt by his easy chair. "So, bad burritos? That's all?"

"Seems so," he said. He smiled at me, and I noticed for the first time how thin his skin seemed. I wondered how old he was. "I saw Cody's truck out there," he said. "Things going well?"

"Rachel Alexandra is fine."

Lew nodded and leaned his head back against his chair. "You should go back out there and finish up with him before he gets away," he said, peeking at me from under half-closed lids. "I can tell we interrupted something."

I began to protest, but stopped. I just patted his arm and left. Outside, I leapt from the steps and ran into Cody who was rounding the corner around that damned bush on his way up to the door.

He seized my arms and lifted me to keep us both from crashing to the ground. "Whoa!" he cried. "Where's the fire?"

"Oh! I wanted to catch you before you left," I said as

he set me down. I felt how close he was and remembered how much closer he had been just minutes ago. I smiled up at him. "I guess you caught me, instead."

He smiled back, but let go of my arms. "How's Lew?"

"Food poisoning. Taco truck."

"Mm-hmm. Have to watch those things." He stepped closer and brushed the stubborn curl off of my forehead. He was close enough to kiss me again, and I ached for it, but a flutter caught the corner of my eye. I looked away in time to see a face disappear from the trailer's kitchen window and a hand drop the curtain back into place.

Cody had seen, too. "Damn," he said.

"What?" I croaked.

"I've got to get a move on," he said, stepping back. "Tell Lew and Molly they can call me if they need anything." He began walking to his truck.

No. Not again. "Cody!" I called. He stopped and turned. What could I say? "Do you want some coffee?"

"I'd better not," he said. "Sick animals and stuff." He scuffed the ground with his toe.

"I see," I said, but I was thinking, *Shit, shit, shit! How can I make him stay?* I knew this was going all wrong, but I didn't know how to change it. I couldn't think at all because it took all I had not to fling myself between him and his truck and tear my clothes off.

Instead, I whispered, "Sick animals."

I couldn't say anything more, and he didn't say anything more, so we didn't even say goodbye when he climbed into his truck and drove down my driveway. I watched him from the spot in front of the trailer's steps until he was out of sight.

Then I sat on the step and watched the alpacas in the barnyard as the sun set.

When it was time for chores, Molly came out and joined me. "Do you want to talk about it?"

I didn't look at her, instead watching the light filtering through the big oak tree that dominated the barnyard. "He kissed me," I said finally. Again, why not be honest?

"Oh, how wonderful," Molly cheered.

"Yeah, it was," I said. "Then he ran away. Again."

"I see."

I turned to look at Molly. "I've been sitting here thinking, and I don't understand him at all."

"I do," Molly said. "He has not had good luck with women."

"Oh?"

Molly smiled and looked at the sunset. "I know you think Lew and I are awful gossips, but I can't really say more than that about Cody's life." She watched the sun a moment and offered, "You could talk to Rosie, though."

"Rosie?"

Molly nodded and then stood. "Come on. Let's get the critters fed so that you can go inside and make some phone calls."

∽∾∽

I sat in front of my TV, not watching a reality show as it blabbered on. Cody's kiss burned inside me still, and

I hoped the chaotic, sadistic drama on screen would distract me. It did not.

The phone rang. Grateful, I turned off the TV and squealed when I read the caller ID. "Nana!"

"Oh, my dear! How are you?"

"Nana," I choked.

"Honey? What's wrong?"

And there I was, thirty-four years old, blubbering to my grandmother about the mess my life was.

I told her about the overwhelming ranch. I told her about the mess at work. I told her about Martin's letter. I told her about Evan's indifference to animals. I told her about Cody's kiss.

And, God bless her, she listened until I was done—quiet, and not even tutting anymore.

"Well, my dear," Nana said. "I can help with the alpaca business. I have lots of experience marketing luxury fiber to specialty markets."

"Geesh. Of course you do. You have fiber goats and rabbits. Why didn't I think of that?"

"You are in a 'DIY' mode, dear. I went through it, too, after your poppy died. But you know you can't, right?"

"Can't what?"

"Do it all yourself. You need help. Everyone does."

I was quiet, so Nana went on.

"As for Martin, he is not a part of you or your life anymore, nor should he be. Burn the letter."

"I buried it in alpaca poop."

"Good. Finally, the boys." I could hear Nana settling

back into Poppy's ratty old recliner. She had taken to sitting in it after he died, even though when he was alive, she had complained about how horrid it was.

"You know, people are attracted to confidence and happiness. I'm not surprised that two people are vying for your attention. You've left the past and you are obviously looking to the future."

"But, what do I do?"

Nana didn't answer. I could hear creaking as she shifted in Poppy's chair, and I felt a sudden pang of jealousy for their long love.

"I can't think of a kind way to say this," she said when the creaking stopped. "But, even though I've never met him, I don't trust this Evan person."

"Nana!"

"I know, I know. But I am having a hard time getting a feel for him. There's something...evasive about him."

This time I was quiet as I remembered all the times Evan had sidestepped questions about his past, his previous relationships. I also thought about his jealous streak.

"Cody seems like a much more honest fellow," Nana said.

I gripped the phone. "So, why won't he come in for coffee?"

"Nice boys don't take other boy's girlfriends," Nana said.

"They don't kiss them, either," I said.

"No, they don't," she said. "But sometimes a quiet knock isn't as effective as kicking the door down. Plus," she added. "Sometimes timing is everything."

"Isn't that the truth?"

ⳍⳋⳍⳋ

I made a lunch date with Rosie for the next day. Evan was disappointed when I cancelled on him, so he insisted that we still have dinner and go to my place that night. I could see a darkness behind his eyes as I left, and, as much as I wanted to treat his jealousy lightly, I had to admit that my lunch with Rosie was tantamount to cheating on him. Not that kissing the vet in the barn wasn't cheating, too.

As I drove to lunch, I wondered why I felt I was cheating when neither of us had made any commitment to the other. I felt like I was betraying some sort of trust, which made me wonder about the kind of person I was. I thought about how Martin had lied to me, and I didn't want to hurt Evan the way I had been hurt.

How did I get into such a mess?

Rosie suggested a Mexican restaurant on the edge of town, "In honor of Dad's botulism burrito," although we opted for the sit-down place, and not the taco truck. I found Rosie seated in a corner, scarfing down tortilla chips as if they were her main course.

"Hiya," she said, brushing crumbs from her shirt. "Thanks for the lunch invite, Meg. It's nice to get away from the ranch occasionally."

"Sure. I wanted to thank you for all your help. With the horses." I slid into the booth and began munching chips, too.

"So what's on your mind?" Rosie asked.

"What do you mean?"

"Oh, don't be all coy with me," she said. "I know you appreciate the lessons and stuff, but I could tell on the phone last night that you wanted to talk about something."

"Have you talked to Molly or Lew today?"

"Tried to. Molly wouldn't let Dad on the phone and she wouldn't say anything." Rosie looked at me and narrowed her eyes. "It's got me curious, I'll tell ya."

I picked up a menu. "Can we order first?"

"Why draw it out? Hit me."

I took a deep breath. "Cody kissed me yesterday afternoon."

Rosie's grin spread across her whole face. "Awesome."

"And then he ran away like the first time I asked him in for coffee."

"Oh." Rosie sat back in her seat and looked out the window.

I waited a moment before I said, "Molly suggested I ask you why. She said that Cody's had bad luck with girls, or something."

"I suppose that's one way to put it," Rosie said. She fiddled with her menu and then looked at me. "You remember that Cody and I had a thing once, right?" I nodded. "He and Bill were good friends at the time," she continued. "I was taken with both of them. Eventually, I had to make a choice, and I chose Bill." She smiled. "I made the right choice. Although both were good men, I loved Bill."

"But Cody—"

"Poor Cody took a long time to get over it," she said. "For years, he felt like he'd lost a friend, which was worse than losing the girl. I suppose he's right."

"Did Bill and Cody make up?"

"Oh, sure," she said. "Even Cody and I became close again. We tried to be a couple for a while after Bill died, but it never felt right, so we stopped trying and remained good friends."

"So, I don't understand how that explains why he kissed me and then ran," I said after a moment.

She shook her head. "Cody has decided that he never wants to compete for a woman again. He's fucked up every relationship he's ever had by backing down when he should have been standing up. If there's even a hint of competition, he disappears." Rosie looked me in the eye. "The fact that he kissed you amazes me because he knows about your relationship with Evan."

"Such as it is," I said.

"What does that mean?"

"I'm pretty confused right now," I said. I put my hands over my eyes and rubbed. "What do I do?"

"Depends," Rosie said. "I doubt you'll get more than a polite hello out of Cody from now on as long as Evan is in the picture. Evan is in the picture, right?"

I nodded. "Coming over tonight."

Rosie nodded. "What are you going to do?"

I shook my head. "No idea."

"Well," Rosie said. "Whether you like it or not, you're going to have to play these balls one at a time. But Cody is smart enough not to wait around forever. And I'll tell you another thing," she said, standing. "I have a bit of a protective streak. I love Cody in my own way, and if I think he's going to get hurt, I'll tell him so. Understand me?"

I nodded and watched her slip on her coat. "What about lunch?"

"I suddenly want to eat at home," she said. She stopped and squeezed my shoulder. "Don't worry, honey. Either way, I like you and you're welcome to ride anytime, okay?"

"Please don't leave," I said. "I still don't understand Cody."

Rosie looked down at me. Then she sat. "Okay, listen," she said. "This is as plain as I can make it. Cody must really, really want you to take a risk by kissing you. That really exposes him, especially since you are Evan's girl in his eyes. Do not expect anything else from Cody. And—" She took my hand. "Stop seeing this Evan person."

"But what if—"

Rosie shook her head. "It's Cody or Evan. You can't have both. You can't play Evan to the end and then expect Cody to be waiting in the wings. If it were me," she said slowly, "I would seriously think about which man I wanted to be with in ten years. That's the man you should be with now."

She stood again.

"You're still going?" I squeaked.

She nodded. "You have some thinking to do, and I need to go for a ride."

"Why?"

She chewed her lip before answering. "Cody and I have been friends a long time. There's been a long string of emotions. Riding helps me think, to process stuff." Then she smiled at me, thank heaven. "See you at your lesson?"

I tried to smile. "Okay. Bye."

I watched her go and once again envied her swinging horsewoman's stride and how her legs were so thin that they didn't fill up her boots. She looked left and then right and then walked away. I ordered a margarita and tried not to cry.

ᘓᕽᘓ

Evan was either suspicious or observant about lunch because over dinner that night he asked right away, "What's eating you, honey?"

I stopped pushing my salad around and tried to look happy. "Just lost in thought," I said, not untruthfully. "Got another pile of shit-work today."

"I'm going to have to talk to the boss about that," Evan said. "I mean, we all get scut work our first couple weeks, but this is ridiculous. You're too good to be doing someone else's grunt work. What a—"

"Don't say anything to Penny," I said, reaching for his hand across the table. "I don't want this to get any worse. I can handle it. The only way to show that I can do it is to work until she gets bored. Right?" I smiled at him.

"No, someone else should be doing this stuff. I'm tired of seeing you used like this. I mean, we can find someone else." He scowled at the door as if he were expecting his arch-nemesis to walk through it.

Why was he so angry?

"Evan," I said. When he looked at me, I said, "I can't be the girl who sends her boyfriend in to fight her battles for her, can I?"

Evan frowned. "I suppose that would look bad, huh? Okay, we'll do it your way. I'll warn you, though. She's a tough kid."

"I'm tougher," I said, trying to believe it.

ɷɷ

That night, after another bottle of wine, Evan kissed me again and again at the foot of my bed. I tried to enjoy it, but I kept comparing his kiss—hungry, anticipatory, confident—with Cody's—tender, urgent, erotic. As Evan buried his head in my neck, I suddenly wondered what it would feel like if it were Cody who was nibbling my earlobes. Then it was Cody who was undressing me and who slid between the sheets with me. I got so caught up in the fantasy that I was surprised when I opened my eyes and found Evan panting on the pillow beside me, instead.

"Jesus, Meg," he said, kissing my forehead. "I like you lots better at your house. What's in that pillow of yours? Pheromones?"

I laughed and thanked the gods that I wasn't the type who screamed names during sex. However, even after a playful shower and more wine, I couldn't sleep. Evan was out as soon as his head hit the pillow, arm curled around my waist. When I was sure he was asleep, I slid out of his grasp and stood looking at him for a moment before slipping on my robe and going to the kitchen.

Tea with milk didn't help quiet my mind, although it was Nana's surefire cure for insomnia. I felt that I had just deeply betrayed someone, but I couldn't decide which man I'd hurt. Maybe I had just betrayed both of them.

Then I got angry. Why was I in this position? I gave up men because they were all such assholes, and now that I was trying to make it on my own, here were the only two non-assholes in the world, and for some reason I had to choose from a pair of seemingly equal unknowns.

"*Fuck*," I said. What should I do? Give up on Evan because Cody gave me the hots? Evan gave me the hots. If I broke it off with Evan, maybe Cody would turn into an asshole, too, just like all the others. Then where would I be? Alone.

I said, "Fuck!" again and threw my spoon into the sink with a clatter.

The sound made me suddenly afraid that Evan would wake up and find me missing, so I rushed back to my bedroom like some pathetic wimp. Evan was still sleeping, his arm wrapped around my pillow instead of me. I slid back into his embrace. Then I stared at the image of us reflected in my dresser mirror. I wondered if that was really what I wanted to see in ten years. I didn't know.

The next morning, I was not as happy as I thought I would be after the first night with Evan at my place. I mean, it was very nice to wake up wrapped up in warm arms and snuggle until my alarm went off at 6:30. Lew and Molly were quiet during morning chores, and I speculated silently about what they must think of me since Evan's little convertible sports car was still parked in my driveway. However, he was very much not in the barn with me. Even my girlfriends had braved the barn one morning of their visit. I felt ashamed of him and of myself, but I couldn't think of what to say to them, so I worked quietly, too.

Lew was not well, anyway. He moved more slowly than I'd seen him go before, and I caught him more than once leaning on his rake breathing slowly, pipe still clenched between his teeth, I expected him to rib me about the man hiding out in my house, but he didn't say a word. That made me feel more ashamed than anything he might actually say, and I retreated to my kitchen after chores as quickly as possible, feeling silly and chagrined at the same time.

Evan, for his part, had helped himself to some coffee and fried some eggs for me. "Morning, Darlin'," he chimed as I kicked off my boots. "Breakfast is ready!"

To emphasize the role reversal, he had even tied on the frilly apron I keep around for laughs. I shook my head as I washed my hands at the kitchen sink and smiled.

I was almost in a good mood when we arrived at work, but that evaporated when I walked into my office to discover yet another pile of files on my desk. I dropped my bags on the floor behind my desk, flipped open the top file, and sighed. It was more of the same crap. I closed the file and flopped into my chair. Something had to change.

I sighed and poked the file on my desk with my finger, willing myself to just get it over with. Evan was right. I felt used. It wasn't just that the things I'd handled at my old job were more interesting, it was that this stuff really was bottom-level data entry. I remembered doing this kind of mind-numbing work when I was an intern. It was insulting to my training to make me perform these monkey-level tasks.

Angry, I snatched the open file. Stupid Penny, insulting my intelligence with this slop. *I'll show her*, I thought. I was going to restructure these files so that they were efficient and money-making as I made her insane changes. I'd impress the hell out of her. Then I would quit in a huff.

I read the file much more carefully than the others and thought about it instead of just entering the changes. These investments weren't as messy as the others. I made a plan that redistributed the funds to balance the investments given the recent uptick in international oil prices. I was pretty pleased with the results, so I made the written changes on the file and then printed it out. I wanted to put the plan into the file and then talk to Penny and maybe the clients before implementing it.

However, I noticed something weird as I read the printout. Naturally, the original numbers and the new ones didn't match because of the changes I had made, but they didn't look right. I pulled out my calculator, the one that had earned its place in my purse by getting me through graduate school, and started crunching numbers. I sat back after several minutes and stared at my trusty calculator because it refused to agree with the new numbers. I always found at least $200 that should be in the account, but wasn't.

I chewed on my thumbnail and wondered what to do. Finally, I turned to my computer and changed the numbers back to the originals. Until I understood this better, I wasn't going to argue with the math. Math was usually right.

The funny thing was that my trusty calculator and I kept finding discrepancies of about $200, but only in some of the files. The others seemed fine. When I had no more thumbnails, I switched to pencils and gnawed two of them down to the lead as I puzzled.

Just before lunch, I had four files open on my desk. They were all off by about $200. They all stank of something rotten. I sat a moment, screwing up the courage to do what I knew was right. I had to see Penny.

I tucked the files under my arm and made myself march to her door. I took a deep breath and tried not to think about her relationship with Evan or how much she must hate me. Something was wrong. I had to report it. I knocked.

"Meg," she cried when I opened the door. "How are you? I never see you!" She stepped around the desk and led me to one of her chairs. Then she leaned against the desk and smiled at me. "How are you doing?"

This was not the reception I was expecting. I perched on the edge of the chair, ready to dodge something. "I'm doing fine," I said.

"I know our little operation here isn't as sophisticated as what you're used to, is it? Do you like the work here?"

How was I supposed to answer that? "Honestly," I said, "I haven't seen an interesting case since the first one you handed me." There I go being truthful again, but what did I have to lose?

Penny twisted a pen between her long elegant fingers. "Really?"

"All that's crossed my desk have been old, tiresome flies that needed updating. Seriously, an intern could have done that data entry. I was bored out of my skull."

Her eyes narrowed slightly. "Was?"

Ms. Alverez is sharp, I thought.

"Today, I stopped making the written-in changes for some of the files and made investment plans for them instead."

"I see," she said. "So you want to present those plans to me now?"

"Actually, no." I took a deep breath. "Something's wrong."

"What do you mean?"

I handed her the files. "I was told to make the penciled-in changes to these files, but after I made the new investment plans for these accounts, I couldn't reconcile the dollar amounts. They were each off by about $200."

"All the files you worked on were off?"

"No," I said. "Only these four. So far."

She closed the file she was looking at. "So you think there are more…discrepancies?"

"These are the only ones I found this morning," I said. "I only started looking today. I have about two hundred files in my office, and I—"

"Two hundred?" Her face darkened. "You shouldn't have that many files. What the hell is going on?" She turned to her computer and after a moment of her nails clicking on the keyboard, she printed a sheet and handed it to me. "Do any of these look familiar?"

I looked at the sheet. "No," I said. "I would have remembered these. They look interesting."

She twirled the pen some more before looking me in the eye. "Stop whatever you're doing and spend the rest of the day documenting the work you've done since you got here," she said. "Make copies of every scrap of paper, every note that you got with those files and try to categorize the kind of work you did. If you have time, make me a spreadsheet with all the fields and what you did with them."

My eyes grew wide. "What are you looking for, Ms. Alverez?"

"Penny," she said. "I don't know, but don't tell anyone about this. Not even Evan."

I blushed at his name, but Penny smiled. "Oh, like it's a secret."

"You're not mad?"

"Mad? Why?"

I felt two inches tall, but I forced myself to speak. "It's my fault for listening to rumors, but I thought you had a thing for Evan. That's why you two fight in your office."

Penny laughed. "That would be something else," she said. "Evan's my great aunt's son. My cousin sort of. He's just grown up in my overly contentious family and feels free to express his opinions to me loudly. I probably shouldn't let him get away with it. He didn't mention that we're related?"

"No," I said. "He's been pretty private about personal details."

Penny nodded. "When he started here, he really didn't want it to be known that we're relatives. He thought that any hint of nepotism would hurt his reputation. Ha!" She laughed again. "Wait till he hears about this rumor."

I laughed, too, mostly in relief. "You have no idea how much this was worrying me."

"No wonder you've been avoiding me. You thought I was sending you the shit work to punish you for stealing my boyfriend."

We laughed and laughed until we both leaned back in our chairs and sighed.

"So," I said. "Somebody has been screwing with me."

"Screwing with us," she said. "The company, you, me. That's why I want to focus on documenting your time here. And really, don't tell anyone."

"You think Evan is involved?"

"No," she said after the merest hint of a pause. "No, I don't. But I don't want him involved, either."

"Sure, I understand."

"I'm really sorry about this," Penny said. "I like you, and this must have been a really difficult couple months."

"You have no idea."

❧

As Evan and I were leaving for lunch, I began to say, "See you in an hour," to Nancy as we passed, but instead, I paused at the door and turned back. "Nancy, do you want to come to lunch with us?"

Nancy and Evan stared at me. Then Nancy blinked. "Oh, no. I bring my own lunch. Plus, I take lunch at two so I can field calls while people like you are out." She smiled sweetly. "But thank you for the offer."

"Another time, then," I said and left with Evan.

"Why'd you do that?" he asked when we were on the street.

I looked up at him, the warm spring sunshine backlighting him. I had asked Nancy to lunch because I realized something while I was cataloguing the files in my office: Nancy was the one who had always brought them to me. She was the one who had said they were from Penny. I opened my mouth to tell Evan all this when I remembered my promise to Penny.

"It seems like a nice day for an outdoor lunch and I felt sorry for her trapped in there," I said. "Where can we eat on a patio around here?"

"I know just the place," he said. "We can even walk."

We turned down the street, and I tried to enjoy the spring, but Penny's suspicions kept churning through my head.

Finally, Evan broke the silence. "What were you and Penny laughing about in her office this morning?" he asked.

"Oh, this and that," I teased.

"C'mon. It's been weeks since you even made eye contact with the woman, and now you two are best friends? What's going on?"

"You're a little paranoid," I said, poking him. "We were actually talking about you, though."

His pink skin turned a little green. "You were?"

"I'd heard a rumor that you and Penny once had a thing, or at least that she was in love with you."

"Eewwww!" Evan recoiled in horror. "She's like my mom's age. We're related."

I laughed. "I know that now."

"You thought we were together?" he asked. "How could you think that?"

I shrugged. "I'm the new girl. I have to work with the information I'm given."

"Who gave you that repulsive information?"

I stopped to think. Where did I hear that? "It seems like that rumor was everywhere, but now that I think about it, maybe Nancy was the one who told me."

"Really?" He glanced over my shoulder at the office door three blocks away. Then he dropped an arm across my shoulders and steered me down the street. "I'll get to the bottom of this."

"I wish you wouldn't," I said. "There's no harm done here, right? Let it go."

"All right," he said. "As long as you don't tell anyone that Penny's my cousin. That would be weird, too."

"Deal."

We ambled to a pleasant pub garden for lunch. I declined a lunchtime brew for a lemonade and tried not to think about Nancy. Not yet. I needed to get back to the office to connect some dots first.

ശ്ചേ

It was equally difficult to settle into date mode that evening, even though Evan and I were sitting in the charming bistro which Evan had declared "our place." My thoughts kept drifting away from the conversation, only partly because he was talking about playing Risk online.

Just before leaving work, I had handed—not emailed—Penny a copy of the spreadsheet documenting my time and the files I'd worked on. I was no amateur, so once I started compiling the data, I could see that something fishy was going on. Penny only had to glance at the first page before she looked me in the eye.

"What do you see here?" she asked.

I shook my head. "I don't know for sure," I said. "But it doesn't look right."

"No, it doesn't," she said. "Keep this under your hat

for now. I mean it. You'll be willing to answer questions if it comes to that?"

"I suppose it depends on the questions, Penny," I said. "But I always try to do the right thing."

Penny nodded. "Have a nice weekend."

ೞೞೞ

"Meg? Are you all right?"

I jumped at the sound of my name. Evan looked concerned and the waiter stood expectantly.

I picked up my menu and pointed at something random. "Number five, please."

"So where were you just then?" Evan asked when the waiter left.

"Work."

"Pah," he said. "So we're at the point in our relationship where work is more interesting than I am?"

I rolled my eyes. "Oh, please," I said. "Nothing is more interesting than your obsession with a board game." I winked.

He gave me the goofy smile he flashed when he was caught. "At least it's something complicated. Not like being obsessed with fluffy animals."

"Not fair," I said and tried to laugh.

"Fine," he said, pushing the candle to the side of the table so he could hold my hand. "You pick the next topic of discussion."

Damn Penny and her gag order. All I could think about was the investigation at work. I so wanted to bounce my theories off of Evan. Instead, I stalled. "Umm, alpacas?"

Now he rolled his eyes. "I guess I walked into that one."

"You're coming over tonight?" I asked. When he nodded, I said, "How about you grab a pair of jeans from your place and you can come out to the barn? Watch us do chores and pet a fluffy creature?"

"Okay, I'd like that," Evan said, even though his face showed that he actually wouldn't. I squeezed his hand as if I didn't notice.

ᆼᘐᆼ

It was almost sunset when we got to the barn, so Lew and Molly had begun chores without me. They were polite to Evan but, not surprisingly, they weren't warm to him. I thought they would be thrilled that Evan had actually joined us for chores, so their coolness stung me. These country people certainly were a loyal bunch.

"This is Missy," I said to Evan as I fed the black alpaca from my hand. "Here, you try."

He held the pellets in his hand and looked at the alpaca doubtfully. "So, she won't bite?"

"Stop being a baby." I laughed. "Put your hand out flat. She doesn't have top teeth in front, so even if she did bite you, it wouldn't hurt."

Evan hung back too far for Missy to reach him, so I pushed him closer. He finally smiled at the feeling of fuzzy lips on his hand. "Tickles."

When we were done with chores, we walked back to the house. "Wasn't that kind of fun?" I asked.

"Sure, I guess," he said. "As long as you don't mind the smell of a barn and getting dirty."

"The fun part about getting dirty is getting clean," I reminded him.

It took him a moment for my comment to sink in, but then he cried, "Race you to the shower."

The next morning, Evan refused to get up and go to the barn with me. "You wore me out last night," he insisted. "The animal scent of you. Rawr." With that, he rolled over and put a pillow over his head.

Lew and Molly had the grace not to comment on Evan's absence. Maybe they noticed how much I didn't want to talk about it. I stood stroking Missy, wondering how in the world he hadn't been charmed, not even a little bit. I tried to convince myself that it might not matter, but I was realizing that it wasn't a little thing to me.

"Not an animal person?" Lew ventured finally.

I looked up and tried to smile. "You noticed?" I gave Missy a final pat, stepped out of the stall, and sighed. "He's never had any use for four-legged creatures."

"Could be a problem," Lew said gently.

"Maybe," I said. "It would be nice if he showed a little interest. Of course, I could give a flip about Risk—it's a game he plays all the time with his friends," I explained. "Couples don't have to have exactly the same interests."

"I suppose that's true," Lew said.

I pretended to dust off my hands. "Time for breakfast," I said with as much enthusiasm as I could muster, and marched out of the barn.

I found Evan in my frilly apron again, making more eggs and bacon. "Sorry I wussed out there," he said. "I made you breakfast." He handed me a plate of food and a steaming mug of coffee. "Does this make up for it?"

What could I say? I kissed him. "This is so sweet."

I ate the food as if I were very hungry. His gesture was at least a gesture. I was also amused by his skinny legs poking out from under my lacy robe and apron. But I still wished he had come to the barn with me that morning. I wondered if he would ever come to the barn again.

Chapter 9

I watched Evan's ridiculous little convertible make its way gingerly down my gravel driveway, standing in my robe, hair dripping, sipping the last of the coffee he'd made. I was still warm from the shower, and I still glowed from the good-bye kiss, but I had to admit that his lack of interest in my animals bothered me a lot. I chewed on my lip as the last wisps of dust settled back onto the driveway. I decided that I could make allowances for his disinterest in my passion if he could make those same allowances for me. That was what couples did, right? Compromise?

Lord knows, I'd compromised enough with Martin.

I drained the mug and went back into the bedroom. Later on, I would help Molly scoop poop out of the fields, but I had a couple hours to myself first. I pulled on my most comfortable jeans, boots, and a sweatshirt, but I decided against a bra since it was laundry day. After I tied my hair back with a bandana, I threw a load of delicates into the washing machine and grabbed the thickest thriller novel in the house. I headed to the barn and found a comfy spot where the hay bales were stacked like a couch with a back and arms to lean on. I began to read to the music of munching, humming alpacas. It was like listening to monks chant.

The Zen-like humming of the alpacas and the spine-tingling novel were just the thing to take my mind off of my problems at work and my problems with men. That was, if you could call my situation "problematic." Well, I supposed I just had.

My heart was pounding, in fact, when the heroine of the novel was going into the room of the haunted house she lived in. Her hand was on the door handle, and an unearthly feeling crept up from under the door, giving her—and me—goose bumps and suddenly—

"Meg?"

I yelped and bobbled my book, which fell to the barn floor. I looked up. "Cody? What the hell?"

He laughed at me. "I didn't mean to sneak up you."

"Again," I reminded him.

He dropped to one knee and picked up my book, glancing at the title. "Ah, I see why you were so absorbed," he said. "This one made me check my closets for a month." He smiled as he handed it back to me.

I fanned through the pages. "I like a good thriller," I said. "I haven't finished this one yet. Does everyone die?"

"It's a bloodbath at the end," he said, sitting next to me on the bale. "Gore central. Do you want to know if the girl gets out alive?"

"Don't you dare spoil it for me," I said. "I'd never forgive you."

"Noted," he said.

"What are you doing here?" I asked. I noticed my heart was still racing, even though I had put the book down. "It's a Saturday morning. Did Molly call about something?"

"I actually just dropped by to see how Lew was doing. But I have to pop inside barns. It's a compulsion, I guess." He looked at the alpacas munching on their breakfast. The older ones recognized him and eyed him suspiciously. "These guys look fat and happy." He pointed at a very round dam. "When's she due?"

I squinted. "Hmm. That's Darla. I think she's due anytime now. She sure looks ready to pop, doesn't she?"

I looked at Cody, who was watching me, not the alpaca, and felt myself flush under his gaze.

"Meg?" he said. "I wanted to apologize for that day—in the barn."

"Apologize?" I croaked. "What for?"

His brown eyes grew deeper and my heart pounded louder. "For kissing you. For—not coming in for coffee."

"You're sorry you kissed me?" I whispered. "Really?"

"Well, no. I'm not sorry for that," he admitted.

"You're sorry you didn't come in for coffee?"

"That, I should have done that. Except—"

I touched his jaw with my fingers before I knew what I was doing. He pulled away a little, but then settled his chin in my hand, just as Missy did when she was content. Then he covered my hand with his own and closed his eyes. He kissed my palm. Then he wrapped his arms around my waist and pulled me to him.

He kissed his way up until he found my earlobe, then across my cheek until he found my mouth. Then he leaned me back across the bale, his hand carefully positioned between my hair and the hay.

He brushed at the errant curl on my forehead as his eyes darted from one part of my face to another. "You are so beautiful."

I smiled and pulled him down again before I could start thinking. His hands felt so warm and right on my sides as he touched me and kissed me. His fingers found their way under my old sweatshirt and tickled as they worked their way up.

Cody stopped suddenly and stared at me. "You're not wearing a bra," he exclaimed.

"It—it's laundry day," I said.

"Really? Laundry day?"

What was happening? I tried to shrug, my shoulders crackling against the hay. "I wasn't expecting company." Cody sat up, so I did, too. "What is it?"

He stared at the barn floor a moment before turning to me and taking my hands. "Please tell me you're single."

For a moment, I forgot to breathe. *Lie!* a voice in my head commanded. "I don't know what I am," I said.

His hands tightened over mine. "You'd cheat?" he nearly hissed. He was watching my face.

I felt myself tear up under his gaze, and I finally looked away. "No," I said.

"So, this would have ended, how?" He took my chin and made me look at him. "How would it have ended, Meg?"

"Jesus, I don't know!" I said, tears sliding off my chin onto his fingers. "I was trying not to think. Not to over-think. Just be!"

"Do you love him?" Cody asked. "If you do, I'll disappear."

"Don't disappear, Cody," I whispered. "Oh, don't do that."

"Do you love him? Meg?"

"It's only been a few weeks. I don't know. I don't know if I love him."

"I love you," Cody said. "I've loved you since the night the cria died."

"Oh." I looked into Cody's face and knew it was true. I also knew that this was not the kind of thing he could lie about. I pulled his hand up to my cheek and settled my face into his palm.

After a moment he pulled away and sighed.

"I'm going to put it all out there, Meg," he said. "I love you. Now you know it. I know you're in a…relationship with this Evan person. I'm willing to give you a little time to decide, but I don't share. If you show me that Evan's your choice, I'll even refer you to another veterinary clinic."

"That sounds like an ultimatum," I said in a small voice.

"I suppose it is," Cody said, scuffing some hay on the floor with his boot. "But I have to survive." He turned to look at me. "God, I could eat you up right now." He flicked the curl on my forehead. "This thing drives me absolutely crazy." He stroked my cheek with his rough knuckles and smiled. Then he stood and walked away, pausing at the door. "Tell Lew I stopped by. You don't need to tell him how I feel about you, though. I'm pretty sure he's figured that out already."

I listened to Cody's footsteps and to his truck starting. I listened to it going down the driveway until the sound was so small that the robins' songs and alpacas' chewing drowned it out entirely.

What the hell am I going to do now?

ଏ∕ଡ∕ର

I was late to my lesson with Rosie, and I couldn't concentrate on anything my mount, Evangeline, was trying to teach me. Finally, Rosie halted us and leaned on the horse's shoulder and looked up at me.

"What's eating you?" she asked.

"Eating me?"

"You repeat the last thing someone says to you when you're upset," Rosie observed. "So, what's eating you?"

I watched my hands fiddle with the reins. "Nothing," I lied.

"Bullshit." Rosie sighed. "Get off. Take Evangeline's tack off, rub her down, and meet me in the office for some coffee. You need to talk more than you need to ride."

I knew Rosie was right before I had even finished taking off Evangeline's saddle. I needed to talk. I was wound up and jittery. But as I smoothed the brush across her chestnut hide in long, sweeping strokes, I began to relax. I focused on pulling the sweat and dirt off of her skin. Finally, I rubbed her with a towel, just to make her shine.

After I led her into her stall, I leaned my face against her shoulder and listened to her breathe. When I looked up, the mare was watching me with a kind, curious eye and blew a contented sigh when I scratched her neck. I chuckled when I remembered how afraid I was of Albert and Evangeline when I first came to Rosie's barn. Then I went to find Rosie in her bare, dusty office.

"So what's up?" she asked, pushing something more akin to battery acid than coffee at me. I sat and bravely took a sip. "It's man trouble, isn't it?"

"How much have you heard?" I asked. I hadn't actually meant to say that out loud, but there it was.

She sighed. "Dad's confused because that guy Evan keeps showing up and spending the night. Especially since that started after Cody kissed you in the barn."

"Right."

"So?"

"You've basically outlined my problem," I said.

"It's raining men, huh?"

"It's a bit of a turn-around for me," I said. "My ex

convinced me that men were scum, and all the dates I had in the city confirmed it."

"But the first two men you meet here convinced you otherwise?"

I shrugged. "I moved up here to be by myself, you know? I wanted something that was mine, my own. I've never done anything on my own. This was supposed to be Meg doing it for herself."

Rosie's brow crinkled. "So why go out with Evan? Or Cody?"

I began to tear up. Then I got mad at myself for tearing up, which made me frustrated, so tears began leaping from my eyes. "I hate being alone," I said. "I like being with someone who makes me happy. I guess I'm weak. I can't even last a month without finding some man to take care of me."

"Hold on," Rosie said. "Nobody says that a girl who can take care of herself has to be all alone. Sweetie," she said, making the word sound comforting, not condescending, "you deserve a nice man who bends over backward to make you happy. Okay? It's not a fault to want to love and be loved. That's what makes us people and not robots." She smiled, so I did, too. Then she leaned forward in her chair and scrutinized my face. "But this is old hat," she said. "Something happened last night, or today, that's upset you again."

I looked at the floor and blushed through my wet cheeks. "How do you know?"

"Majored in psychology in college. Or I'm psychic. Never could keep those straight. What happened?"

I took a deep breath. "Cody dropped by this morning and—gave me an ultimatum." That was close enough to the truth.

Rosie nodded. "I see. So you have to choose. By when?"

"He didn't say."

"Do you love him?"

"Who?"

"That's a good question," she said. "Either of them."

"I don't know."

"Of course not," Rosie muttered. "If you did, you'd know what to do."

"What should I do?"

This time Rosie shrugged. "I can't tell you what to do. I can tell you I've got my money on the dark horse because I care about him. But I don't know what would be best for you."

I sighed.

"I'll tell you, again, though: Cody isn't going to wait around forever. He's got too much pride for that. Plus, he won't let himself get too emotionally involved until he's sure you won't hurt him."

"Too late for that," I said. "He told me today that he loves me."

"Oh my God." Rosie threw herself back in the chair. "Really? That's huge."

"I know," I said. "I could tell."

"Does Evan say that to you?"

"Oh, no. But it's only been a couple months—"

Rosie waved to cut me off. "You have a week or two

at most," she warned. "Cody doesn't just say those words over and over hoping that someone will respond."

"He said he'd disappear."

"He will. And it won't take much for that to happen."

"What will it take for him to stay?" I asked.

Rosie examined me like she'd found me on the bottom of her boot. "End it with Evan."

"What if that's a mistake?"

Rosie was suddenly looming over me in a grand impression of someone who was over five feet, two inches. "Jesus, Meg," she cried. "If you were my daughter, I'd slap you. What makes you so incapable of taking a risk?"

She glowered at me, and I felt as if I'd shrunk to the size of a dried mushroom. I stared at my hands, thoroughly ashamed.

"Aw, fuck." Rosie knelt at my side, putting her hand on my knee. "I'm sorry, Meg. I keep forgetting about your shitty husband. Of course you're afraid of being alone, and of commitment, and of being hurt. I'm sorry. It's just that—" She rested her head against my shoulder. "Cody is my friend, and I think you might make him happy. I want him to be happy so badly, and since I can't make him happy myself, I guess I was hoping I could help you two be together."

I leaned into Rosie, taking comfort from her body like I did with Evangeline. "It's okay," I said. Then I stood with a sigh and moved to the door.

"Meg? What are you going to do?" Rosie stood next to my empty chair.

She had resumed her normal size, but I realized I wouldn't want to make her really angry.

"I don't know," I said. "I have to figure that out." I left, pulling the door closed with a quiet "click."

❧❧❧

I attacked my garden on Sunday. I spent hours and hours on my knees, clawing through the beds. I pulled weeds, mowed the lawn, and planted some vegetables. I had a general idea of what I was doing garden-wise since Nana had schooled me in Horticulture 101 the summers I'd spent on her farm as a kid. I still called her on my cell as I stood with my shiny new hedge clippers in front of my defenseless boxwood.

The sun was warm, but clouds streaked across the sky breaking up the heat with little respites of gray shade as Nana coached me in reviving the neglected hedge. When we were satisfied that I had done more good than harm, she turned the conversation.

"How are you doing up there, honey? Do you like it?"

"Yeah, I do," I said. I sat in the freshly mown grass, not caring about getting my ass wet or grassy, and basked in a sudden sunburst. "It's nice up here. I wish you would visit."

"Oh, not until I get my own garden in," she said. "Spring is the busy time, dear. Wait until after the cherries are done in June. Then I'll come up."

"Deal," I said.

"So, how are the boys?" she asked.

I knew she didn't mean Seabiscuit or Secretariat. This was Nana at her most delicate. I could almost smell her if I closed my eyes. "Well," I said. "Things are a bit more complicated now. Cody told me he loves me."

"That's wonderful," Nana cried. "Congratulations!"

"Thanks."

"Wait. You don't sound thrilled."

"Oh, I am," I said. "It's just…"

"That Evan boy is still sniffing around?"

"He's…" How do you tell your grandmother that your boyfriend is sleeping over? Luckily, I didn't have to.

"I see. So you and Evan are sleeping together."

"Yeah."

"For how long?"

"A couple months."

"Well." I heard her shifting and imagined her settling into her creaking porch swing. "Based on what you've told me, if I were you, I'd drop everything and throw myself at the vet."

"You'd what?"

"Strip naked the next time you see him and say, 'I'm all yours! Take me now!'"

I laughed. "Oh, Nana. You would not."

"Would too," she said. "How do you think I got your grandpa to notice me?"

"That's not an image I wanted in my head, Nana," I said.

"Oh, you young people," she clucked. "As if I weren't ever twenty-two, wild, and reckless."

"Okay," I said, trying not to think about my naked grandmother. "Why would you have me throw myself at Cody?"

"He loves you," she said. "What more do you need than that?"

"But Evan—"

"Evan. Pooh."

"Nana. You don't even know him."

"Neither do you," she said.

"I do, too."

"You do not," she said. "I've listened to you and you don't know anything about him. What you do know is that he likes having sex with you—" Here I blushed deeply. "—and that he will never move onto your ranch with you."

"I don't know that," I said. "He might."

"He won't." She said this with finality.

I let her words sink in. I knew she was right.

"I don't know Cody, either."

Nana sighed. "You know the people who love him, right?"

I thought of Rosie, Lew, and Molly. "Yes."

"Has any of them said a word of warning to you about him?"

"Only that he won't wait for long."

"There you go. No references and no history versus glowing references and declarations of love."

"But I don't want anyone to get hurt."

Nana sniffed. "Then you're a fool, too," she said. "Someone always gets hurt. And if you're not careful, that someone is you. Just do your best not to hurt the wrong people for the wrong reasons."

"Okay, Nana," I said, feeling fourteen again. "I love you."

"I love you, Meg," she said. "I'm sorry if I'm impatient with you, but I'd hate for you to lose an opportunity to be with someone who truly cares for you because you are with someone who seems to care for you. Don't be the one who gets hurt this time, honey."

☙☙☙

Monday morning, I found an email labeled red for "urgent" in my inbox. It was from Penny and all it said was, *Come see me in my office at your earliest convenience.*

I turned off my computer, a habit I'd started the week before, and went straight to see Penny.

She waved me in, even though she was on the phone. She pointed to a chair, so I sat. Penny said, "Indeed?" three times before thanking the caller and hanging up. Then she turned to me. "How are you today?" she asked.

"I'm fine. How are you?"

"Good. Good weekend?"

"It was good. Evan and I went out, and he spent the night at my place on Friday," I said.

"Did you say anything about our…situation here?"

"No," I said. "It would have been nice to talk to someone about it, but I didn't even tell my nana when she called."

Penny looked relieved. "Good," she said. "I believe you. Let me show you something."

She handed me a folder. Inside were pages and pages of color spreadsheets tracking transaction on the accounts I had been handling. After studying them a moment, I asked, "What's the column on the right with all the red?"

Penny nodded. "That is the question of the day," she said. "That's the difference between what should be in those accounts and what actually is. It's what you pointed out to me, and what is actually missing."

"I'm not stealing from you, Penny," I said.

"I'm not accusing you. But somebody is stealing."

"Who?"

Penny regarded me a moment with her unreadable face. "I'm not at liberty to say. But I'm really, really pissed off about it, and I want to see them punished. The best way you can help is to not say anything to anybody."

"What should I tell people we've been talking about?" I asked.

Penny flipped thorough a drawer in her desk and handed me a file. "This is the Kennedy-Smith account. It's complex and the Kennedy-Smiths are notoriously finicky. It's yours. It's like a free pass to my office because you're under orders to double-check every single move with me beforehand. Understand?" She winked at me.

"I understand, boss." I smiled at her and stood to go, tucking the thick file under my arm.

"One last thing." Penny came around her desk and put a hand on my elbow. "Be careful with Evan. His wife had good reasons to leave him."

I froze. "What good reasons?"

She shook her head. "Let's just say that his imagination gets away from him sometimes. He's family, so I won't say any more out of respect for my aunt. Just be aware that he's always planning his next move."

"Like playing Risk," I said.

"Exactly." Penny laid a finger beside her nose. "That's exactly what I mean."

∽∾∽

I was exhausted mentally and physically when I dragged myself into my house after chores that night. I shed my clothes and ran a bath. I had just settled in to bubbly heaven when my phone rang. "Yes?" I answered curtly without looking at the caller ID.

"Hi, honey, can I come over tonight?"

Who is this? My heart fluttered for the moment it took me to peek at the name on the phone. Evan. Damn.

"Really?" I said. My disappointment changed to irritation. There went my quiet evening alone. "I mean, I'm getting ready for bed."

"What are you wearing?"

I could hear the lust in his voice, and I could picture the grin on his face. "I'm in the bath," I said.

"Want some company?"

"Not really."

"Aw, come on," he purred. "You can't be too tired for some snuggling."

I had to agree. I wasn't too tired. But I was thinking

about Cody. My heart hadn't steadied from the hope that he was calling me, not Evan.

"Tempt, tempt, tempt, tempt," he whispered. "What's holding you back? I'll make it better."

"Okay." *I know. I'm stupid and weak.*

"Stay there," he said. "I'm on my way."

I sighed, set the phone down, and sank back into the bubbles. Why couldn't I say "no" to Evan? Was it his smooth, freckled body? His impishness? His self-assurance? I was abruptly taken by how different he was to Cody. Cody had thick hair on his head and was not nearly as smooth-chested as Evan. He was not over-confident like Evan, but he did express his desire intensely. Plus, Cody oozed integrity from every pore while I often wondered what Evan was thinking. It was weird that I was attracted to both of them.

The bath was cool by the time I heard Evan open the unlocked back door. He entered the bathroom naked. "Hello, beautiful," he said dropping his pants on the floor. "Let me warm you up some."

At least I knew what he was thinking at that moment.

⁂

We woke to an awful, loud banging on the back door.

"Stay here," I said to Evan as I snatched my robe from the hook and darted to open the door. I found Molly panting on the porch.

"It's Darla," Molly said. "Baby's on the ground and

not breathing. Call the vet and get out here. We need your help."

"Right." I shut the door and ran to my phone, which was charging in the kitchen. I dialed Cody's pager and bounced on my toes until he called back. I answered on the first ring. "Cody!"

"Yes, hello?" He sounded sleepy, and I wondered what time it was.

"It's Meg. Sorry to call so late—early."

"Meg?" He seemed more awake. "I'm always happy to hear from you."

"It's Darla. Her new cria isn't breathing. Can you come? Quick?"

"Oh. Oh! Yes. I'll be there right away."

When I hung up the phone, I heard Evan behind me. "Who's Cody?"

He stood at the kitchen door, wearing only jeans. His blue eyes were darker than I remembered. I wondered how long he had been listening.

"The vet," I said. "You met him at the lunch that one time." I tried to push past him to get to the bedroom, but he caught my arm. "Let go. We have a sick cria."

"Aren't vets like, 'Doctor So-and-so,' or something?" he asked. "You called him 'Cody.'"

"That's just what Lew and Molly call him," I snapped, trying to hide my guilt and panic. "Let go of me. I have to get out there to help."

He held my arm and looked at me so darkly that I was afraid. I resolved not to show it, though, and stared back at him. "Let go," I said again.

He grinned at me. "Sorry!" he said, throwing up his hands in mock surrender. "Just asking."

A few minutes later, I sprinted into the dawn on my way to the barn just as Cody's truck pulled into the driveway. We looked at each other for a moment and silently agreed to put everything but the sick cria to the side. We entered the barn at the same time to see Darla, a big white dam, standing miserably by as Lew and Molly massaged a tiny little life, trying to convince the white baby to breathe.

"What's up?" Cody asked as he and I stepped into the stall.

"Dystocia, we think," Molly said. "But it was over when we opened the barn door. The baby was out and wet but not breathing well. It must have just happened because there's no placenta yet."

"We've been giving mouth-to-snout and oxygen," Lew reported. He pointed to the tiny oxygen tank at his side.

"Good. Let's take a look." Cody flipped his stethoscope over his head and popped it into his ears. He listened to the baby's chest and neck and belly. He took its temperature. Finally he stood up. "Do you have a hot water bottle?" Molly nodded and ran back to their trailer. "We need to get this little guy to the vet school at OSU," he said.

"What's wrong?" Lew asked.

"This is more than a failure to thrive," Cody said. "I think a plasma transfusion and maybe some more diagnostics would help a lot." He looked at me.

"It's not another birth defect?" I asked, my heart banging in fear.

"I don't think so," he said. "The baby is term, and everything sounds right, I actually think he's just worn out from a very long, difficult birth. Look how tired Mom is." He pointed at the drooping Darla. "He needs a lot of support, but I think he'll make it."

Molly ran back in with clean towels and a very hot water bottle. Cody expertly wrapped the little creature into a cria burrito and handed it to Lew. "Let's go," he said.

Lew shook his head and handed the bundle to me. "I can't go," he said. "I feel too rotten. Meg can go."

I scanned Lew's face and indeed, he looked drawn and pale, especially in the dim dawn light. I cradled the tiny creature with his drooping neck to my chest and turned to Cody. Cody glanced at me, then scooped up the oxygen tank and turned to leave. I followed.

As I climbed into the cab of Cody's truck, which was littered with scraps of paper and fast-food drink cups, I heard someone calling my name. I looked up to find Evan, again in my robe, holding two coffee mugs.

"I made coffee and cinnamon rolls are in the oven!" he called.

Shit. "I have to go with the vet," I called back to him. "It's an emergency!"

Cody started the truck, so I ducked in and slammed the door shut. I almost looked back, but just then the truck lurched forward and hit a pothole so the baby's head bounced on the seat beside me. "Oh, baby," I cried and cradled the little neck in my arms. I held the tiny oxygen mask to his face as I'd seen Lew doing and stroked his perfect little ears. I concentrated so fully on the cria that I didn't notice Cody's dark eyes glaring at the road, although I did wonder if he always drove so ferociously.

Oregon State University had one of the few alpaca and llama veterinary programs in the country, and I had heard Lew and Molly talk about how lucky we were to be only a half-hour drive away. I didn't feel so lucky when I finally realized that Cody wasn't driving fast only because he was concerned about the sick cria breathing wetly in my lap.

He hadn't said anything since we'd left the barn. I replayed the events leading up to me sitting in the hostile air of the truck.

My heart sank when I remembered the image of Evan in my frilly pink robe holding coffee in my driveway.

"Cody?" I said when I couldn't stand the silence any longer. "Are you mad?"

He glanced at me, his eyes flashing. "Why would I be mad?" he growled.

"He just kind of showed up last night," I said.

"Don't," he said. "I don't want to know."

"I just want to tell you that I've been thinking about you, us—"

"And he just showed up and spent the night last night. I hear you." Cody swung around a corner so forcefully that I gathered the cria more tightly into my arms to keep it from sliding.

"Please, give me another chance," I said. "I'm not ready to let you go."

"But you're not ready to let him go, either," Cody said. Pain was sharp in his voice.

"Please," I said. "Give me whatever time limit you want. I'll follow it. But let me figure this out in my own way until then." I was afraid to touch him, so I clutched the baby animal to my chest and hoped.

He looked at me hard again, but his eyes softened before he looked back at the road. He made a turn into a parking lot and turned off the key. He turned to me and looked into my eyes. "A week," he said. "One torturous week, and I'm done."

I nodded, afraid breathing would break this reprieve.

"Let's go. We're here."

Lew and Molly had called ahead, and a team of students was waiting for us when we entered the lobby with the drooping cria. I handed him off to a student in coveralls and the vets and Cody disappeared into the back. Before he left, Cody gave me a quick hug. "We'll do our best," he whispered into my ear before leaving.

I sat in the waiting room, staring at pictures of mares and foals frolicking in pastures strewn with buttercups. When I realized I hadn't eaten breakfast, I had some free coffee with extra sugars. I was antsy, jittery, and worried and would have paced if I felt I could trust my feet and legs to carry me across the room and back. So when Evan showed up at the waiting room door an hour later carrying the still-warm cinnamon rolls and a thermos of my coffee, I was truly, truly grateful to see him.

He set the food down and caught me in his arms as I dissolved into tears. When I calmed down a little, he asked, "So what's going on here?"

"I don't know. They just took him into the back and I haven't heard anything. How did you get here?"

"Those people who live at your place, Missy and Newt, right? They told me how to get here. I kind of had to twist their arms, but here I am. Want some breakfast?"

I devoured two rolls without coming up for air. Evan squeezed my shoulder and excused himself. "Your coffee is good, but it goes right through me."

I stared at the bathroom door and realized that this situation summed up my problem: Cody was trying to save my animals, but that was his job. Evan had made a huge effort to help me, but Nana's words and Penny's warning haunted me. I couldn't help but wonder if they weren't wrong.

Then the door to the clinic opened and Cody came out. I stood and met him as he came around the reception desk. "Cody?"

"It was touch and go there," he said. "But he's got some fight in him. He's had a plasma transfusion and that perked him up some. I think the little guy's got a good chance of pulling through."

"Oh, thank you!" I cried and threw my arms around him, laughing with relief. He returned my embrace and kissed the top of my head.

Then I heard Evan from across the room. "Who the hell do you think you are?"

I turned around in Cody's arms and then threw my

hands up between them. I could feel Evan's fury as he came closer. "Evan," I began.

Evan shoved me aside and then punched Cody in the face in one movement, so that we both sat on the floor at once. But while I sat too stunned to move, Cody launched himself at his attacker's knees, knocking Evan down. The two grappled on the floor.

I had never seen two men actually fight before, and I was fascinated and terrified by their fury and strength. I looked up at the reception staff who were leaning over the counter watching the fight with mouths agape.

For a long while, it seemed like Evan had the upper hand, using his long body and the high school wrestling moves he'd bragged about. He had Cody nearly pinned three times before the smaller man wriggled loose and punched and kicked. Finally, Cody landed a huge upper-cut to Evan's chin and knocked him flat on his ass. Cody scrambled to his feet and glowered at his opponent.

Evan tried to sit and say something, but blood poured from his mouth.

"Oh, God." I scuttled over to Evan.

A receptionist appeared with a handful of tissues, which we used to mop up the blood.

When I looked up, Cody stood over us, panting like a bull, blood smeared across his face from cut over his eye. He glared at Evan. When he looked at me, his face changed, softened, but pain and fury crossed his face like a wind whipping through a tree. Finally, he went back into the clinic, slamming the door after him.

Holy shit. I stood, tissue hanging from my hand.

Evan whimpered. "Meg?"

I looked down at him, the wad of tissue in his mouth saturated. Blood was starting to drip from his lips again. His eye was swelling, and he managed to look pitiful.

"Meg, help me."

I sighed and, kneeling, took his head into my lap. "Could someone get some more gauze? I think he's broken a tooth or something."

∾∾∾∾

When things calmed down, a vet student declared that Evan had bitten his tongue, but didn't need stitches. Cody was nowhere to be found. I drove Evan's ridiculous car back to my house with Evan in the passenger seat

He was as sullen on the way home as Cody had been on the way down, but I didn't have a baby alpaca in my lap to clutch. Instead, I glared out of the front window and didn't speak, just as Evan glared out of his window and didn't speak.

Finally, I turned to him. "What the hell?"

"What do you mean, 'what the hell?' What the hell to you," he said. "That man was kissing you."

"He gave me good news, I hugged him because I was grateful," I said, not lying.

"And then he kissed you."

"On top of the head," I pointed out. "Like your grandma might." I really couldn't argue this point any further because even though the kiss probably looked innocent, I knew it wasn't.

"I kiss you on top of the head," he said. "I don't want anyone else doing that."

"You don't have a right to dictate who kisses my head and who doesn't," I said. "You've never made any commitment to me!"

"Neither have you," he said. "Now I know why."

"Don't you think you overreacted?" I said, steering the argument away from Cody.

"No, I don't," he said.

"Well, I do." I turned into my driveway. I jumped out of the car as soon as I was close to the house. "Thanks for the fucking cinnamon rolls," I yelled and slammed the door. Then I ran inside. I could hear the rooster tail of gravel his stupid car spewed as he sped off my property and possibly out of my life.

I flung myself onto my couch and just trembled for a while, waiting until my hands stopped shaking before I sat up and looked at the clock. It was 10:30 in the morning, and it was a fair bet that Penny had realized that I wasn't going to come in today, but I decided I needed to call, anyway. I reached for my phone and dialed Penny's direct line, even though I knew the protocol was to call Nancy.

"Meg? Where are you?" Penny sounded worried and rushed.

"I'm at home," I said. "I had a farm emergency, and I don't think I'll be in today. It's been a terrible morning."

"Mine has been terrible, too," Penny said. "Are you sure you can't come in? I really need to talk to you."

I hesitated, then asked, "Is Evan in yet?"

I heard the phone receiver brush against Penny's shoulder as she moved to look out the sidelight window of her office. "I think I see him walking in now. Boy, he looks like hell. What happened?"

"Can I just come in during lunch and see you?" I asked.

"My God, Meg. He didn't hit you, did he?" Penny asked.

"No, no, not exactly," I said. "But you were right about his…imagination."

"Lunch is fine," Penny said. "In fact, it might be better to talk outside the office. Let's just meet somewhere."

Noon found me dressed in clean jeans and a "Saturday" shirt, seated across from Penny who, though dressed impeccably as always, looked strained across her eyes. Penny's mouth drew a hard, thin line across her face. After we ordered, her shoulders slumped and she rested her head in her hands a moment.

"Penny?"

"Aw, Meg." She sighed. "Those files you were working on? They're the center of a pretty expansive fraud scheme."

I felt the color drain from my face. "Fraud? Jesus. Am I in trouble?"

"No." Penny looked up at me. "Not you. Every way we've crunched the numbers, you've always come out clean. You did exactly what you were told, you did better than could have been hoped, given your instructions. The fraud points elsewhere."

"Oh, good." I sat back, but didn't relax. "So what happened?"

"It seems that in each stack of twenty or so files you were given, about three were designed to funnel money out of one account into another, central account. Do you remember *Office Space*? The scam where they scraped fractions of pennies off of thousands of accounts? Well, this is about the same, except the scraping involved a few hundred at a time. The files were so old and the clients so dense that no one noticed."

I was quiet a moment. "So, as the new girl, unfamiliar with the accounts, I wasn't supposed to notice the differences, either."

"Right. And maybe they expected you to be like other new hires, inexperienced and maybe a little timid. They were banking on you not speaking up even if you caught something." Penny paused a moment. "What made you look at the accounts so closely?"

"I was pissed off by the shit work. I thought I'd show you what I could do, then quit."

She nodded. "I'm not surprised. Like I said, I never give those files to new people. I abuse interns with that stuff." She fingered her napkin before saying more. "You know, I went on a hunt to figure out who was shepherding the files to you."

"Nancy," I said. "Nancy was the only one who ever gave me work. She said they were all from you."

"She's also the one who started the rumor that I had a thing for Evan," Penny said.

"What does that have to do with anything?" I asked.

Penny examined my face, and I felt like squirming. "Honestly, Meg, did he hit you?"

I shook my head. "No, but he walked in on me and my vet as we shared an innocent hug. He shoved me out of the way and had a fistfight with the vet."

"God, really?"

"The vet clocked him and stormed out," I said. "But Evan's convinced that something was going on."

"Was there?"

I looked across the table at Penny. "No, nothing like what Evan pictured, anyway," I said. "Certainly nothing that deserved an all-out brawl in a waiting room. Why?"

Penny regarded me a moment longer. "I think Evan might be involved in the fraud, too."

"Involved?"

"Yes," she repeated. "We think he and Nancy are partners."

"Partners?" I shook my head as I realized I was repeating things. "Why are you telling me this?"

"We think that his job is to keep you off-balance and give you a confidant so that Nancy could gauge which files she could pass off onto you."

"So the rumor about you and Evan was to keep me from confronting you about the workload."

"Right." Penny's face softened. "I don't think the plan was for Evan to actually develop feelings for you. But I think he has." She reached across the table and put her hand on my arm. "I'm sorry, sweetie."

I willed myself not to cry as I looked up at Penny. It didn't work.

Tears fell as I asked her, "Why are you telling me this?"

"I need your testimony," she said. "I want to see them punished, even though it's going to kill my aunt. I need you to make that happen."

"Certainly," I said before I covered my face with my hands and cried.

⋘⋙

I thought I had made it to Penny's office door undetected. I wrote a statement for Penny to include in the investigation and signed it. Then I left, but I wasn't two steps out the back office door when Evan grabbed my elbow from behind and spun me around to face him. At first, his face was ominous, covered in bruises from the fight. Maybe he saw the fright in my eyes because his look softened. "Hey, I'm glad I caught you. I didn't think you were coming in today."

"I wasn't," I said, pulling away. "Penny needed to talk to me."

"About what?" His smile pulled his puffy lips away from his teeth a little. The effect was nightmarish.

"Work." I took a step backward. "I told her I wasn't feeling well, which I'm not. I want to go home, Evan. Goodbye."

I turned and took two quick steps before Evan caught my arm again and spun me around. This time he didn't let go and the dark look didn't go away. "What did you talk to Penny about?"

"I'm not at liberty to say," I said as firmly as I could, though I was nearly shaking with fear.

"Meg, let's get out of here. Let's go down the street, I'll buy you a drink and explain some things."

I glanced around. We were alone in the parking lot. "I don't want to go."

"This way." It wasn't a suggestion, and Evan dragged me around the corner past the front door of the office to the little bar on the corner. He pushed me into a booth near the back and squeezed in next to me. "This is about Nancy, isn't it?" he hissed.

"Nancy?"

"Nancy!" Evan's surprise made me follow his eyes. He was looking at the door to the bar where the actual Nancy Frost stood, silhouetted by the bright daylight outside. She heard her name and came directly to our table.

"I wondered where you were going," she said sweetly. "You passed by the front door in such a hurry. Not even a wave."

"Nancy, get out of here," Evan said through his teeth. "I'm handling this."

"Well, no, honey," Nancy said through a forced smile. "You are supposed to be handling this, but you are obviously not handling this at all."

"Handling what?" I asked.

Nancy slid into the booth across from us. "He's about to explain why you got all that extra work from Penny, weren't you, my dear?"

"Why are you calling him 'dear'?"

"She's blackmailing me," Evan said.

"He's my lover," she said.

"With that," Evan cried, waving a finger at her. "She's delusional. She thinks we're a couple and threatened to tell everyone that we were involved unless I helped her."

"Helped her do what?" I asked.

Nancy smiled in a way that made me feel six years old, which made me furious. "Sweetie," she said. "It would be really stupid of me to tell you what we've been up to since you've obviously sung to the boss already."

"I don't know what you mean," I said, wide-eyed. "Really, I don't. What the hell are you two going on about? Evan, are you really sleeping with her?"

I tried to sound more hurt than scared. I let my frightened tears fall, hoping they would mistake them for tears of betrayal.

Nancy and Evan exchanged a look. Then he put his arm around me and cuddled me up next to him. "No, sweetheart. She's an evil bitch who makes up lies about people. I've been trying to get her fired, so she's trying to ruin my life. Get out of here, Nancy," he hollered.

Nancy stood. "Bitch, huh? I could think of a few names for you, asshole being the kindest," she sniffed and sashayed out of the bar.

I let Evan buy me a drink, but I insisted that I just wanted to go home. He walked me to the car and kissed me goodbye.

"Do you forgive me?" he asked.

"For what?"

"For this morning. For the fight. For Nancy?"

"I'm sure it was all a big misunderstanding," I said. I climbed into my car, but as I drove away, I could see him standing in the parking lot, watching.

When I got home, the first thing I did was lock all of my doors and windows. Then I got the mail and made a huge gin and tonic. I didn't care that it was only two o'clock. It was hours before evening chores, and I wasn't going back to work. I sipped it and watched the home improvement channel. None of the pretty gardens made me feel calmer.

I tried to putter a little to take my mind off the fist-fight in the clinic, the revelation of Evan's character, Nancy's plot to use me to commit a crime. I washed some dishes, including a sticky pan that smelled of cinnamon, and flipped through the mail.

That's when I found a hand-lettered postcard, which had been dropped, into my mailbox without a stamp. It was a referral to another veterinary clinic.

I stared at the wall and realized that I was so over-whelmed that I couldn't even cry over Cody's loss.

Chapter 10

*A*t least this day can't get any worse, I thought as I mechanically sorted the rest of the mail.

I knew better than to tempt fate like that. At the bottom of the pile was another hand-written note. This one was from Molly. I unfolded the paper expecting a report on the sick cria. We'd arranged for Lew and Molly to take Darla down to the clinic so the baby could nurse. Instead, I found this:

> *Meg,*
> *I have to take Lew to the hospital. It's not his stomach, it's his heart. Rosie is sending someone today to take Darla to the cria at OSU. We're at the county hospital in Salem.*
> *We'll call if there is any news.*
> *Molly.*

I almost forgot my purse on my way to my car.

When I arrived at the hospital, Rosie was standing outside of Lew's room talking with a doctor. I stood aside until they were through. It was hard not to eavesdrop. When the doctor walked away, I went up to Rosie and put a hand on her arm. "How is he?"

Rosie smiled a little. "Stubborn," she said. "Too stubborn for his own good."

"What happened?"

"The short story is that what he's been telling everyone is indigestion was actually a series of little heart attacks."

"Oh, no. Did he know they were heart attacks?"

"He thought maybe," Rosie said. "His doctor warned him a long time ago that this sort of thing might happen. He knew the signs, but he refused to give up that damned pipe or eat right."

"What happened today?" I asked, shaking a little.

"He and Molly were loading Darla into the trailer. They had to chase her a bit and he got winded, then he really couldn't breathe and was in a lot of pain. Still, Molly had to clobber him to let her call nine-one-one. Stubborn old man." She smiled at me. "Thank you for coming."

I gave her a hug. "Of course. Can I see him?"

"Yeah, he's awake and feeling pretty good now. Follow me."

The hospital room was brightly lit and the television was on, even though no one was watching it. Molly sat in a chair by Lew's side holding his hand. He was even paler than I remembered and looked very slight without his overalls and dirty farmer's cap. I had never liked hospitals, and seeing this shadow of Lew in a wispy gown and thin sheets hooked up to tubes and wires didn't improve my opinion at all. Molly smiled and stood up when she saw me.

Lew turned his head. "Meg," he cried. "You didn't have to come. I'm doing fine."

I took his hand, but he pulled me down for an astonishingly strong hug. "Of course I had to come," I said as he smushed my face into his pillow. "Had to see how you were doing."

"Such a fuss for a lot of nothing," he grumped, but he hugged me even tighter. Then he lay back in his pillows and caught his breath.

"How are you feeling?"

"Bother," he grunted. "I'm so tired of answering that question. I feel like hell, Meg, pardon my language. I want to talk about something else. Anything else. Something really distracting." The familiar glint in his eye was back. "I know," he said. "Evan gave us the third degree until we gave him directions to the University vet clinic. Did he ever show up there?"

I glanced around the room. Had that really only been this morning? Molly and Rosie were leaning in to hear and Lew was grinning wickedly. None of them had heard anything. I knew I wasn't going to be able to avoid telling the tale, but at least I was among friends.

"I'll tell you," I said. "But only because you're sick. Evan did find us."

"Oh, goodie," Lew said, sitting up a little in bed.

"What do you mean, 'us'?" asked Rosie.

"Well, Cody had just come out to tell me that the cria would probably be fine, and I was so grateful that I hugged him. Cody kissed the top of my head. That's when Evan came out of the bathroom."

"Oh. Was he mad?" asked Rosie.

"You could say that," I said. "He sort of attacked Cody."

"There was a fight?" Lew laughed. "God, this is better than I thought."

"They were fighting at the clinic?" Molly asked.

"It was pretty vicious," I said. "Finally, Cody clocked Evan and flattened him."

There was a general cheer. "That's my boy." Lew chuckled. "So, he won?"

"He doesn't think so," I said. "I went to help Evan because he was bleeding, so Cody stormed out. I found this in the mail tonight." I pulled the vet referral card out of my purse and gave it to Lew.

"Aw, geesh," he said. "We saw you arguing with Evan when you got home."

I felt myself tear up and sniffle. "Yeah, Evan's turned out to be an asshole in more ways than one," I said.

"So, you went from two men to none in the space of one day," Rosie said.

"That pretty much sums it up," I said. "Are you mad at me for messing things up with Cody?"

She put an arm around my waist. "I'm disappointed

things haven't worked out," she said. "I'm sad for you and Cody. I think you two could have been good together."

"Meg," Lew said. "Do you want Cody or Evan?"

"Cody."

"Why?"

"Because he loves me. Because I love him," I managed to say before I crumpled into Rosie's shoulder, sobbing.

"Hush. We know you love him. We know you do," she cooed.

When I calmed down, Lew sat up in bed. "Meg," he said. "You want Cody? You need to go get him."

"Get him?" I sniffled. "I couldn't—"

"He's done," Lew said. "He's not coming to you anymore. That's what this means." He waved the blue card.

I looked at Rosie who shook her head. So did Molly.

"Oh, but—"

"No 'buts' about it," Lew said. "You need to go get Cody. Find him someplace he can't get away. Corner him. Make him listen. Tell him you love him. Tell him Evan's gone. Meg," he said, taking my hand. "It's the only thing. If you don't do this soon, he's going to make it a project to forget you. I've seen it before."

Rosie nodded. "It's not pretty, and it takes years to wear off."

"And wear something cute," Lew said. His grin told me he felt better.

୧୭୧୬

I had a late night at the hospital visiting with Lew and Molly and Rosie and did chores on my own not only that night, but the next morning, too. I was so tired after chores that I was on automatic pilot. I was out of the shower and putting on pantyhose before I realized that I didn't want to go to work. I looked down at myself—showered, fully dressed, missing only makeup and coffee—so I decided to go in, anyway. I couldn't hide from Evan and Nancy forever. Plus, I really needed to tell Penny in person what had happened in the alley and at the bar yesterday afternoon.

So, instead of going to my office when I arrived—late—to work, I went directly to Penny's office.

"Great," Penny said when I stepped across her threshold. "I'm glad you're here. You're just in time for the fireworks."

"Fireworks?"

"Do you know that you repeat things when you're nervous?"

"Yes."

Someone knocked on the door. Two men in suits entered and closed the door carefully behind them.

"These are Agents Donaldson and Standard from the State Attorney General's office," Penny explained. "This is Meg Taylor."

"Donaldson. Pleased to meet you," the tall one said, shaking my hand. "I understand you're the catalyst for all this."

"Cata—I suppose I am," I said.

"Well, we're ready, ma'am," Agent Standard said to Penny.

She nodded and picked up the phone. First she called Evan and then Nancy and asked that they each come to her office right away.

Evan arrived first, smiling brightly until he saw me sitting in a chair next to Penny's desk. "What are you doing here, Meg?" he asked.

There was real fear in his eyes when he saw the other two men. Instead of answering, I bit my lip and tried to swallow the lump in my throat.

Then Nancy walked in, already suspicious. She took in Penny, Evan, the detectives, and then her eyes fell on me. "You told me that you hadn't said anything to Penny."

I tried to act calm and confident. "I lied to you. How does that feel?" Penny raised her eyebrows, so I said, "On the way home yesterday. I'll fill you in later."

Evan looked like he was going to have a panic attack. He started glancing at the door, but the tall detective had stepped between him and the exit. "Mr. Ridgefield. Ms. Frost. You are both under arrest for fraud and conspiracy to commit fraud."

"What the hell, Meg?" Evan cried. "You bitch! You sold me out." He took a step toward me, but the detective snatched him back and had him handcuffed before he got any closer.

"I probably want to press charges of my own for battery," I said, suddenly angry. "I have witnesses from an incident yesterday."

The detective nodded and called for backup because Evan was still swearing and fighting. Nancy was not handcuffed, but the detective was still standing by the door. It was plain she wasn't getting away. She sat next to me in a chair and crossed her ankles demurely.

"You know," she said quietly to me. "We picked you because you seemed pliable and stupid."

"Stupid?"

"That's right," she said. "I could just tell that you were the kind who wouldn't confront her boss and wouldn't question being punished for a lover's triangle." Nancy leaned forward, and I swear, her pupils were slits, like a snake's. "You were the perfect patsy."

"Shut up, bitch." Penny was standing. "You were outsmarted by your own patsy. Now who's stupid?"

The door opened. Three plain-clothes policemen stepped in and led Evan and Nancy out.

"I'm going to tell my mom about this!" Evan hollered over his shoulder as they dragged him out.

"Please do," Penny called. "You can break her heart instead of me."

Then it was very quiet in Penny's office. The outer office was in utter turmoil as Evan was dragged through the cubicles protesting his innocence and kicking chairs and desks as he passed. After they were gone, the whole office was buzzing.

Penny called her assistant and told her not to let anyone inside her office.

"We'll just hide out in here until things calm down," she said to me.

I was sitting in the same chair, hands clasped. I hadn't moved since I sat down.

എഐഐ

Over the next hour, I told Penny about the cria, the fight at the vet's office, my encounter with Evan and Nancy in the bar, and Lew's trip to the hospital.

"Jesus, what a wretched day," Penny said.

"Do you need me here now?" I asked. "I want to go home and hide under the covers."

"No, I don't need you," Penny said. "Just keep your cell phone nearby. I'm sure the police will want a statement from you at some point."

I stood and smoothed my skirt. "Thank you, Penny."

"For what?"

"Well, honestly, if this whole fraud thing hadn't happened, I might have actually ended up with Evan."

She nodded. "You're welcome."

"Why did his wife leave him?"

Penny didn't miss a beat. "He pushed her around some and then cheated on her with Nancy."

"Oh."

"Meg, I'm sorry I couldn't say anything, but I was hoping that he had changed. I thought he and Nancy were over. I'm so sorry that this happened."

"It's all right," I said. "Honestly, from the beginning he reminded me of someone, but I couldn't put my finger on who until just now."

"Who?"

"My ex-husband," I said. "They are both charming, handsome, and excellent liars."

Penny smiled. "Then you're due for a change. Do you know anyone who isn't an excellent liar?"

This time I smiled. "I do." I said. "And I even know where he might be."

&ന&

Okay. So I had never actually been to Cody's clinic before.

Thank heavens for GPS.

I followed the directions to Cody's veterinary clinic. I passed the unassuming building twice before I turned into the parking lot. Until I saw the sign out front that read *Mid-Valley Veterinary—small and large animals, Dr. Arden*, by the driveway, I had assumed the building housed a fly shop or real estate office. I parked out front and sat in my car for a moment.

The weight of the past couple days settled into my lap, and a rush of "what ifs?" appeared in my head. What if Cody won't see me? What if he was on his way to see me and I miss him? What if Cody decides that a woman who just shows up and throws herself at him is too pushy? What if he rejects me?

I leaned my head on the steering wheel for a moment and closed my eyes.

Come on, Universe. Give me a sign.

What came on the breeze through my open window was the scent of sweet hay and animals from the stable behind the clinic. The smell took me right back to my own barn and then to the time Cody kissed me on the hay bale. I remembered he smelled of hay, of animals and sweat, and a hint of clean soap. I remembered how much I had wanted him and how safe I'd felt as he laid me down. I really, really wanted to feel that way again. With Cody.

I sat up as I realized that as much as he loved me, he meant to cut me out of his life. We'd never be together unless I stood up and found him, now. As I grabbed my purse and opened my car door, the lady in my GPS cooed, "You have arrived at your destination."

A receptionist sat behind a desk and smiled at me. "May I help you?"

"I need to see Cody—Dr. Arden," I said. "Now."

"Oh, he's in with a patient," the plump, smiling woman said. "The sweetest little kitties! If you'll have a seat, I'll tell him you're here."

"I can't wait," I said. "I'm sorry." I pushed through the door labeled *exam rooms* and ignored the woman's protests.

There were only two rooms. One of the doors was open and the room was empty. That made it easy. I opened the other door. Inside I found Cody holding the cutest cat ever—the lady in front was right—and in his other hand was a syringe. A basket of similarly adorable kitties sat on the exam table, with a family and a little girl of maybe four watching. "Um, I'm here to help Dr. Arden. It looks like you have your hands full," I said, closing the door behind me.

The family looked from me back to Cody who held the squirming kitten. He didn't move, so I got a good look at his bruises and the stitches over his eye. He looked so banged up, I wanted to scoop him up and make it all better. I ignored the blood banging in my ears, stepped forward, and gently took the kitty from his hands. After a moment that seemed impossibly long, the barest hint of a smile crossed his lips. He deftly gave the kitten its shot.

We gave the other four kitties their shots and the grateful family left, thanking Dr. Arden and his "assistant." When the door closed after them, I stood in front of it and turned to face him. My head whirled when I looked at him.

His dark eyes flowed fluidly between desire, anger, and pain. He looked caught halfway between pouncing on me and running away.

Finally, he swallowed hard and leaned against the metal exam table. "Why are you here, Meg?"

"I got your card."

"I gathered that much," he said, dropping his gaze to his hands. My heart thrilled a little when I realized that his nails were gnawed down to the quick like mine were. "Why are you here, in my office?"

"I—I want—you," I stammered. I wrapped my arms around my waist hoping that I could literally hold myself together just a little longer.

"No, you want Evan," he said, shaking his head. "That much was pretty evident yesterday morning."

"Oh, Cody," I said. "He was bleeding."

"Evan certainly wants you," Cody said, rubbing his bruised jaw.

"No, he doesn't," I said.

Cody looked up.

"He and his partner were arrested this morning for fraud. They were using me as a front for a skimming scheme at work." I swallowed my shame. "Evan was using me."

"He didn't fight like someone who was just in it for the money," Cody said.

"Maybe Evan had feelings for me," I said. "But he's such a good liar that I couldn't tell. Just like my rotten ex-husband." I sat on the one chair in the exam room. "I can't tell when someone is lying to me."

He shifted his feet. "I don't lie to you, Meg."

I looked up at him. "I know."

"How do you know?"

"I just do. I trust you. I've trusted you since the first time we met."

"You just said you were too trusting," Cody said with a small smile.

"No, I said I can't tell when people are lying to me," I said. "There's a difference. I couldn't tell when my ex, Martin, was lying, but I trusted him. I would have followed him to the ends of the earth. I couldn't tell when Evan was lying to me, but I never quite trusted him. Something always told me to hold back. I didn't trust my hunches. That was a mistake." I looked up at him again. "I trust you, and, I know you won't lie to me."

"So Evan's out of the picture?"

"He's not even on the radar anymore."

"This is my opportunity to swoop in and be the second choice, then?" he asked.

I could feel him pulling away again. *Damn.*

I stood and took a step toward him. I felt so light-headed and scared I could barely stand, so I held on to the metal table as I stepped around it. "Cody, I've just told you that I made a huge mistake trying to be with Evan. I just told you that he is a liar, a cheat, and violent—well, you saw that yourself." I stepped closer. "I've also just told you that you are the only man that I have trusted since my marriage dissolved. I know you won't lie to me."

"Not enough," Cody whispered, but he didn't move away.

I took a deep breath and stepped even closer. I touched the buttons on his shirt, lightly tracing their roundness, feeling his chest rise with his breath. I could feel his heart pounding though the fabric as clearly as I could hear my heart in my ears. "I love you," I whispered and lifted my eyes to his.

"How do I know?" he asked. Hs voice cracked. "You might be so lonely that you would say anything to have a man around."

"That's what you think of me?" I bit the inside of my cheek. *Don't cry. Don't cry.*

"No, not at all." He touched my arm. "But—"

"I've loved you since the night I threw you out of my house," I said.

"What? Why then?"

"Because you did the right thing, even though I was hoping you wouldn't. That showed me that you would always do the right thing. I've never dated a man with integrity. You have so much, it's intoxicating." Cody took me into his arms and pressed me to his chest. I melted into him and sighed. "Can you forgive me for taking so long to realize how perfect you are?"

"I can forgive you anything," he whispered. "Let's get out of here."

"How about lunch?" I said, peeking up at him.

He kissed me. "I'm not hungry." He took my hand and led me out of the exam room. "Liz," he said to the receptionist. "I'm going home—sick. Reschedule everything. Bye."

I waved to the astounded Liz as Cody led me out the door.

෧෧෧

Hungry or not, I insisted on lunch. We went to a cafe up the street and ordered sandwiches. Cody kept his arm firmly around my waist until we sat at a table outside.

He pushed his food aside when it came and kept holding my hand. I used my other hand to hold my turkey club for a bite.

"I could watch you eat all day," he said.

"Why aren't you eating?" I mumbled with my mouth full.

"Not hungry," he said. "Why are you eating?"

"I don't want to make the same mistakes. You know, take things slow. See what happens."

Cody shook his head. His hair lifted in the breeze. "I don't want slow," he said. "I love you. You love me. What else is there to wait for?"

I looked at my sandwich a moment.

"Why did you come to me today?" he asked.

"Lew said that if I didn't, you'd disappear."

"Lew was right." Cody plucked a pickle off of my plate and chewed it slowly. "So if he hadn't told you to find me, you wouldn't have?"

"No, I would have." I took his hand. "It just might have been too late."

"We owe him a lot, then."

I nodded.

Cody touched my face, and I felt like soaring over the clouds and doing backflips.

"Are you going to eat that?" he asked. When I shook my head, he said, "Then let's go."

❧❧❧

We almost didn't make it to Cody's place. There were some long stoplights when one or the other of us would reach across the bench seat of his truck, and we'd kiss until someone behind us would honk. Eventually, we made it to his small house with a tidy yard and green shutters.

"What do you think?" he asked.

"I think it's the best place in the world."

Cody led me through the house, but he didn't slow down for a tour. Instead, he led me straight through the house to his bedroom. The bed was not made, but everything else was in its place. As he laid me down, he smiled. "This is a bit better than a hay bale, isn't it?"

I grinned. "I don't know. I think we'll have to test that out later."

He laughed and brushed the curl out of my eyes. "This thing drives me crazy."

"Show me how crazy," I said before pulling him down and kissing him.

The first time we made love it was animal and about hunger and lust. We tore the sheets off the bed and flung our clothes everywhere.

The second time was tender, trusting, and delicious. We looked into each other's eyes. I touched his skin. We moved in slow symphony.

The third time was just plain fun.

Finally, I rolled over from dozing and was seized by a deep hunger. I nudged Cody. "Let's shower and find some food."

"Mmm. Shower," he muttered and reached for me again.

"I mean it," I said. "I'm hungry. One bite of turkey sandwich wasn't enough for all this…exercise."

"Okay."

Wet hair dripping, we found a quiet Chinese restaurant and had an early dinner, seated side-by-side in a booth so we could feel each other's legs pressed together. After we'd drunk our tea and laughed over our fortune cookies, Cody leaned back and sighed. "Oh," he said, "by the way, the cria and dam are doing just fine. I checked on them this morning. He should be coming home in a day or two."

"That's wonderful," I said. "Lew and Molly will be happy to—" Then I sat up straight. "Oh, my God. Lew!"

"Lew? What's wrong with Lew?"

"He's in the hospital! Come on. We have to go see him."

I filled Cody in on Lew's heart attacks as we drove into town.

"Why didn't you tell me before?"

"I was kind of distracted," I said.

He squeezed my knee.

こうこう

We found Lew alone in his room, looking ill. He perked up when Cody and I stepped into the room hand-in-hand.

"Jesus," he cried. "Look at you two! If I didn't know better, I'd say you'd been together for years."

Cody stepped forward. "I understand I have you to thank for this," he said, offering his hand.

Lew shook it. "The courage and desire were all hers."

"The idea was yours," I said to Lew. "If it weren't for you, I probably would have just wallowed in pity and shame until it was too late. Thank you."

"Glad I could help you kids," he said.

"How are you doing, old man?" Cody said gently.

"Been better," Lew admitted. "Gotta take some pills and quit the pipe, they say."

"You'd better do what they say," Cody said. "We need you around."

"Damn straight you do," he said. "Think of what might have happened if I hadn't been."

"I prefer not to," I said, leaning into Cody and enjoying the feeling of his arm around me.

Epilogue

April the next year:

For one brief moment, the clouds broke open and my lawn was flooded with the glorious weak yellow of April sunshine. This lasted long enough to lure a few of my hardier Oregon-bred guests onto the patio with their drinks to bask in the warmth like optimistic lizards. And being of Northwest stock, they stayed outside long after the sun disappeared, impervious to the chilly gray spring weather.

Beth and Margot chose to stay inside in the kitchen where they helped Nana and me put the finishing touches on lunch for thirty people.

In January, I realized that the one-year anniversary of my moving to Oregon was approaching, so I decided to throw a party. Then Cody took me to a rodeo on Valentine's Day—apparently a family tradition—and proposed by slipping my cold hand into his coat pocket and sliding the ring onto my finger.

So the party morphed into an engagement party, too.

As I put the last piece of chicken on a platter, the ring glinted at me, and I smiled. As if on cue, Cody slipped in to the kitchen and hugged me from behind.

"The natives are restless," he said.

"Shoo," Nana said. "We're nearly done."

She flapped a dishtowel at him in exactly the same way she used to chase Poppy out of the kitchen. Nana had practically adopted Cody on the spot.

Rosie, unlike Cody, was permitted in the kitchen, and she was soon loaded with plates of sandwiches and heading for the buffet in the dining room.

I sat next to Cody with my plate of Nana's fried chicken, and he squeezed my knee before taking a huge bite off of a drumstick. Across from us, Lew and Molly were deep in a discussion with Penny about terriers, of all things. The shared passion surfaced when I mentioned Lew and Molly's new pup to Penny. She nearly turned inside out with glee when she realized they all had the same kind of dog. Said black-and-tan balls of energy were currently lurking under the buffet tables, taking every opportunity to steal food.

Today, as most days anymore, Lew had a pink toothpick tucked behind his ear as he ate. When he wasn't eating, the toothpick was a proxy for his pipe, which he'd eventually given up after his stent operation and subsequent hospital recovery finally convinced him that he needed to stop using tobacco. I missed the smell of perfumed pipe smoke, but not enough to mention it to Lew. I liked him much better than smoke wreaths, no matter how comforting.

Of course, seeing Penny made me think of Evan. During the trial, I felt immense guilt when I thought of Evan sitting in a cell serving time for fraud. Cody eventually cured me of this with his gentle, insistent reminders that I hadn't done a damned thing to Evan to feel guilty about.

The trial would have been worse if Cody had not been sitting beside me the entire time, holding my hand like an injured bird.

I snapped out of this memory when I saw Cody's mom waving to me as if she had just seen me from across a parking lot. I smiled and waved back. Cody's whole family had made the trip down from Montana for the party, parking their enormous bus-sized RV in our lawn so that Mom and Nana could sleep in my guest room. It had taken me all morning to convince my mother to skip the heels she had brought for the party. She stood in her calf-high boots, instead.

I hoped she was careful about where she stepped outside, but at least her shoes wouldn't sink into the lawn.

Cody's parents—still in mushy love after forty years—were deep in conversation with Nana about gardening. I could tell by the looks on his brothers' faces that some hijinks were in the works for after dinner.

I hoped there wasn't a repeat of the "snake incident" that happened when I was visiting at Christmas.

The sun reappeared after lunch, so we all grabbed lawn chairs and blankets and adjourned to the pastures with iced teas in hand.

Cody and I cuddled on a blanket next to Margot and her partner Peter who was warming to the idea of buying a farm to grow organic vegetables.

Beth was gamely trying to sit on a damp blanket in her pretty dress while balancing a very full glass of tea. I didn't have to warn anyone not to spread their blankets onto a pile of poo.

The alpacas emerged from the barn and noticed the people in their field. They began ambling down to investigate because sometimes visitors to the pastures had apple bits in their pockets. Today, the visitors also had baby carrots.

Then a shot like white lightning flashed from the barn and raced toward the party. Smarty Jones drew up before he actually ran over anyone, but no sooner had he stopped, then he turned on his heels and raced up to the barn again, slowing only to do a bouncy antelope impression alpaca people call a "pronk."

"I think he's feeling better than when I first met him," Cody said and smiled.

I remembered the weak white bundle on my lap that awful day when Evan attacked Cody in the emergency vet's office.

"I feel a lot better since then, too," I said, leaning against him.

Then a faint rain began to fall, so soft that, instead of fleeing *en masse* inside, everyone in the pasture turned his or her face up to the sky. I felt the tiny drops fall on my face like kisses, and, not for the first time since I met Cody, I felt perfect.

About the Author

Maren Anderson is a writer, teacher, and alpaca rancher who lives in rural Oregon. She writes while her children are at school and spends the rest of her time scooping alpaca poop, knitting, playing with her family, reading, and watching cartoons and nature programs on television. She teaches literature and composition at a local college and novel writing to eager, budding writers. If you want to know more about Anderson's writing, novel classes, or alpacas, contact her via Facebook (https://www.face book.com/MarenBradleyAnderson), onTwitter (@maren ster), or at http://www.marens.com.